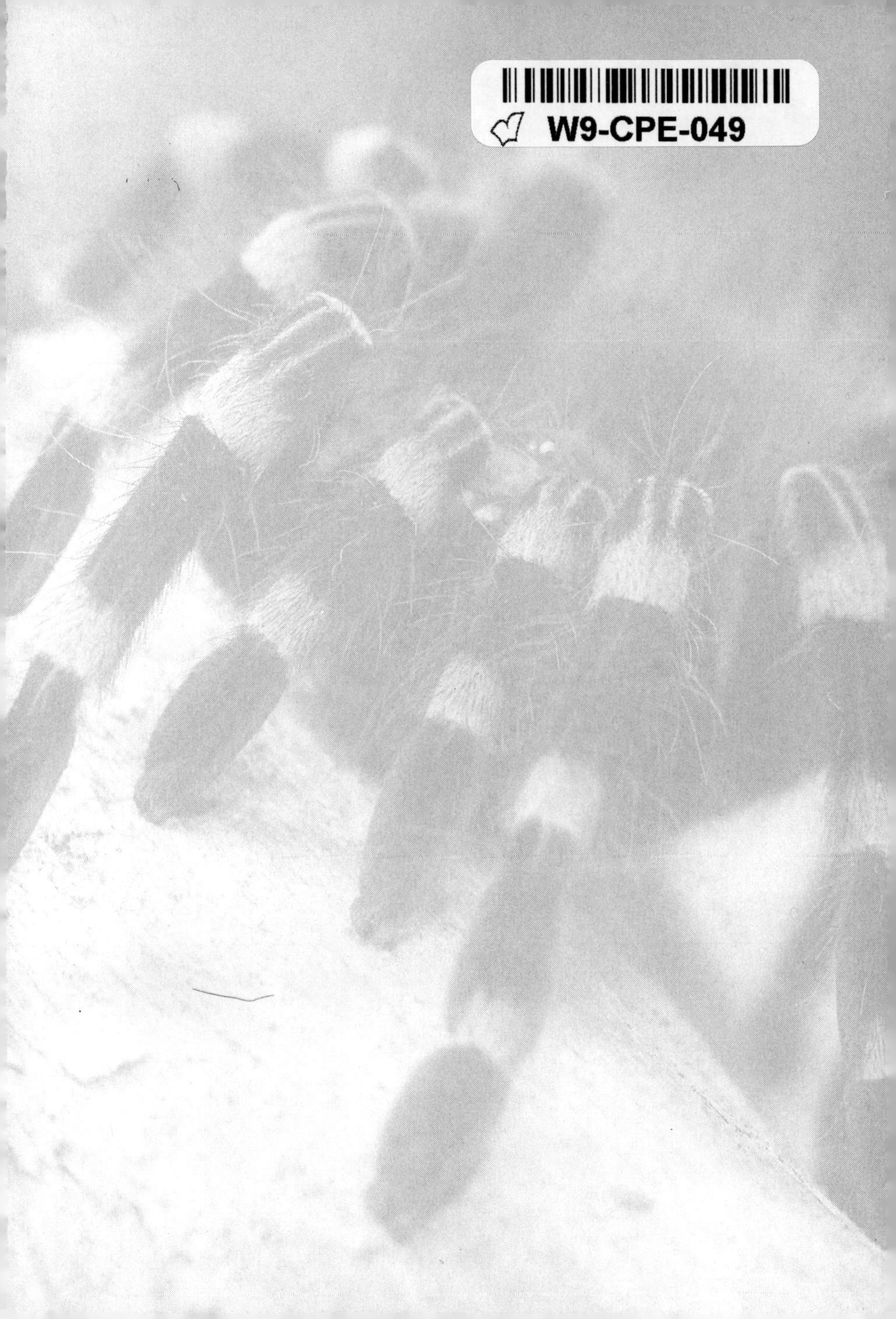

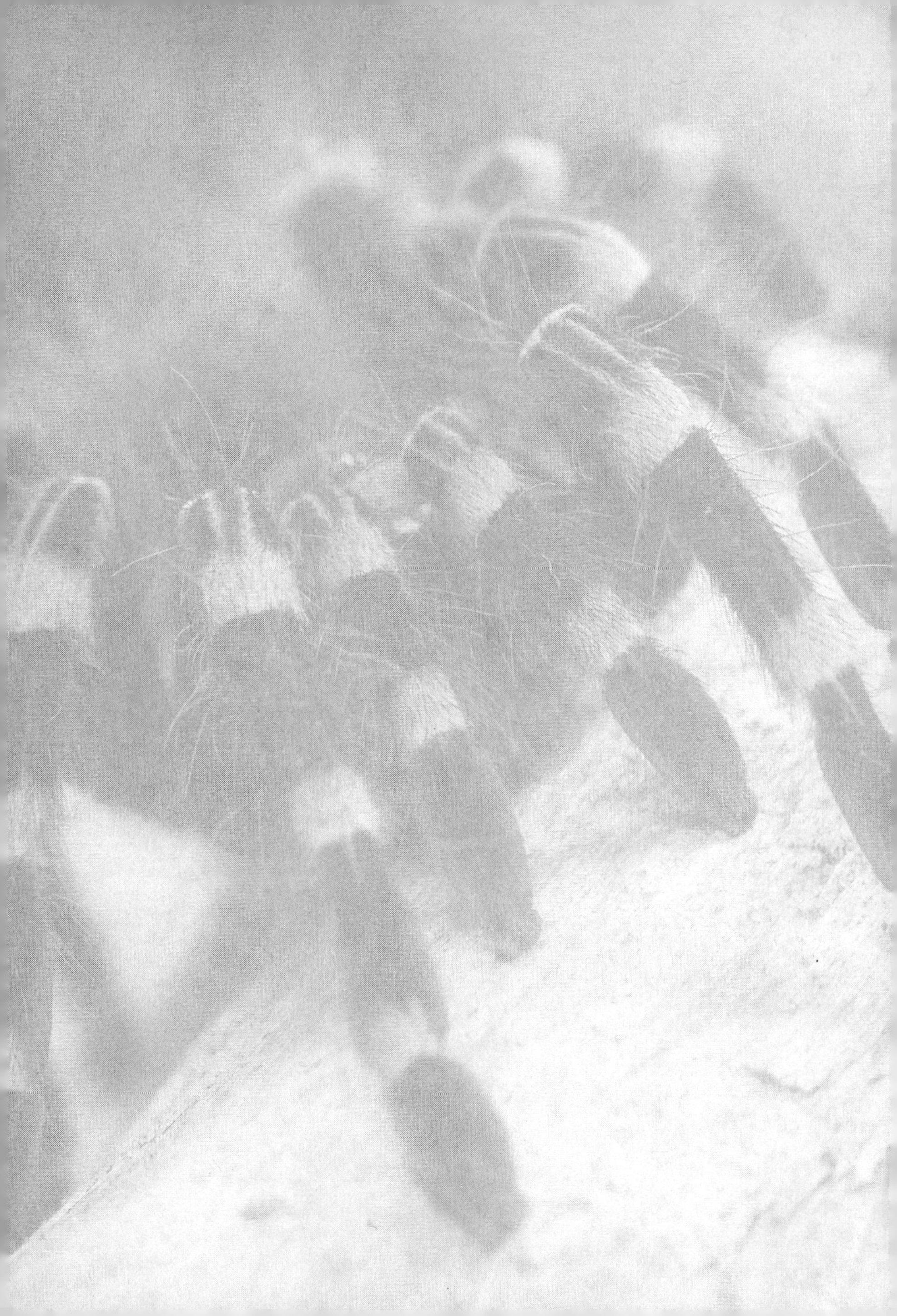

THE MYSTERY OF THE

TARANTULA TRAP

by Carole Marsh

Published by Gallopade International/Carole Marsh Books.
Printed in the United States of America.

First Edition ©2014 Carole Marsh/Gallopade International/Peachtree City, GA
Current Edition August 2016
Ebook edition ©2014
All rights reserved.
Manufactured in Peachtree City, GA

Managing Editor: Janice Baker
Assistant Editor: Whitney Akin
Cover and Content Design: John Hanson

Gallopade is proud to be a member and supporter of these educational organizations and associations:

**American Booksellers Association
American Library Association
International Reading Association
National Association for Gifted Children
The National School Supply and Equipment Association
Museum Store Association
Association of Partners for Public Lands
Association of Booksellers for Children**

Once upon a time …

Papa said …

That's a great idea!
And if I do that, I might
as well choose real kids as
characters in the stories!
But which kids would I pick?

MiMi,
PiCK ME,
PiCK ME!

Christina

ME TOO,
MiMi,
PiCK ME,
TOO!

Grant

MiMi,
ME TOO!

PAPA,
TELL MiMi
TO PiCK ME!

Avery

Ella

MiMi,
DON'T
FORGET
ME!

Evan

You sure are characters, that's all I've got to say!

Yes, you are! And, of course, I choose you! But what should I write about?

National parks!

SCARY PLACES!

Famous PLACES!

FUN PLACES!

Disney World!

New York City!

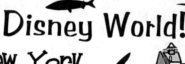

Dracula's Castle

GRAND CANYON

Write one about spiders!

We can go on the *Mystery Girl* airplane ...

I can FLY US anywhere!

Mystery Girl

Or aboard
the *Mimi!*

Mimi

Take me to the
Forbidden City!

Or by surfboard,
rickshaw,
motorbike,
camel ...!

I can put
a lot of **history,**

mystery, science,

legend, lore, and **laughs** in

the books! It will be educational and fun!

Good
stuff!

8

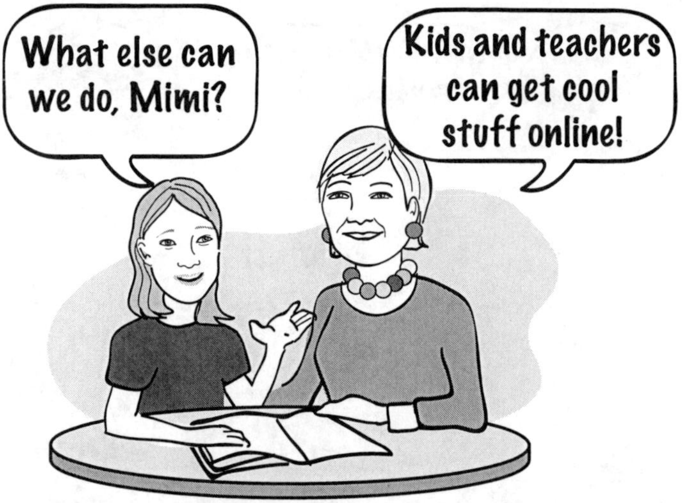
What else can we do, Mimi?
Kids and teachers can get cool stuff online!

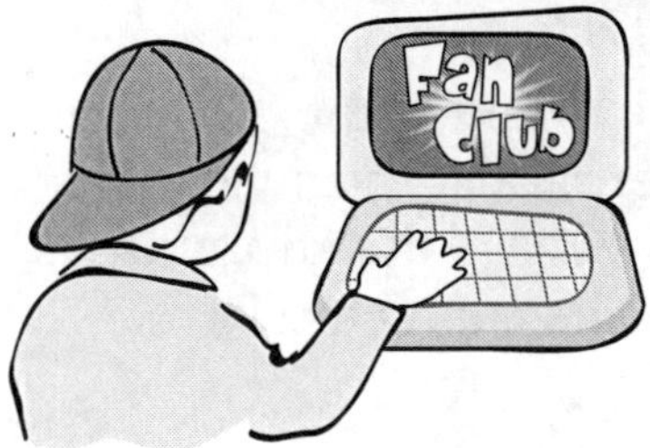
Fan Club

Can we have a Fan Club with photographs and videos?

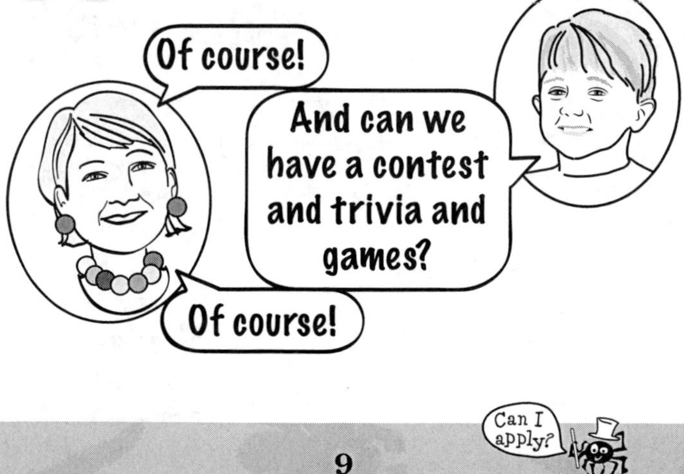
Of course!
And can we have a contest and trivia and games?
Of course!

And so, join Mimi, Papa, Christina, Grant, Avery, Ella, Evan, and Sadie aboard the *Mystery Girl*—where the adventure is real and so are the characters!

START YOUR ADVENTURE TODAY!

READ THE BOOK!

GO ONLINE!

TRACK YOUR ADVENTURES!

MEET THE CHARACTERS!

www.carolemarshmysteries.com

A Note from the Author

WHO LOVES TARANTULAS?

Maybe the answer to that question is: only another tarantula?! A lot of people are big fans of spiders, but NOT ME! That's probably because—like snakes—I can't tell the good spiders from the bad. Maybe spiders get a bad rap, but maybe they deserve it? Or not?

My first experience with a tarantula was when I was a little girl growing up in Atlanta. My sister Suzy and I had turned over the picnic table in our backyard, and using an old sheet for a sail, we were "playing pirate." My little sister looked down at the ground and bent over to pick up a "fuzzy rock." She held out her hand and opened it. When she did, a VERY LARGE tarantula stuck out all its legs! (Maybe it was just stretching? Or showing off? Or warning us to beware?) All I know is that he was pretty cute...did not bite...and marched off across the yard!

You will learn a lot about spiders—maybe even enough to love them, or at least respect their role in the ecological balance of the world—in this book. So join me on this amazing arachnid adventure that's full of creepy, crawly surprises!

— *Carole Marsh*

1

ARID-ZONA

Evan squinted his eyes into a tight, thin line. "Man, I'm roasting!" he said, cupping his hands above his eyes to shield them from the sun. His stick-straight blonde hair looked bleached white in the bright September afternoon.

"Ahh, the desert," Mimi said. She dabbed the sweat from her forehead with a scarlet handkerchief decorated with dainty white flowers. "Remind me again why we thought this was a good idea, Papa."

"Insects!" Papa boomed in his deep Southern drawl. "You said you had to see the desert insects. And just for the record, I never thought it was a good idea." Papa winked at Avery and Ella, who nodded in silent agreement.

Mimi and Papa had invited their grandchildren Avery, Ella, and Evan to travel with them to Tucson, Arizona, to explore a new city for a few days. Their baby sister Sadie stayed at home with their mom and dad. Mimi was a famous children's mystery writer, and often traveled across the globe to do research for her books.

This time, she wanted to visit the University of Arizona. She had spoken to a professor in the **entomology** department to help her learn about the local insects and related creatures she wanted to include in her newest book. So Papa had loaded Mimi, the kids, and Mimi's giant red suitcase onto the *Mystery Girl* airplane and flew the crew all the way to Tucson.

On the flight in, Papa pointed out the steep, rocky mountain ridges that rimmed the desert valley below. In the valley sat a bustling city, with towering silver skyscrapers and jam-packed highways.

"This here is Tucson, Arizona!" he announced to the kids through the microphone attached to his pale green headset.

Once they landed at the airport, the kids were surprised at the desert environment around them.

"It's so flat here!" Ella said, scanning the scenery. Strands of shoulder-length blonde hair stuck to her upper lip like a mustache. Little beads of sweat built up on her forehead. "I guess those mountains fooled us!"

"And so hot!" Avery added. "But it feels dry, not sticky like at home." She pulled her long blonde hair off her neck and tied it into a ponytail.

"Now I know what a turkey feels like!" Evan said.

"What are you talking about?" Ella asked her little brother.

"You know, on Thanksgiving!" he said. "I feel like a turkey roasting in the oven!"

"The heat here is different from what we're used to," Mimi said. "In the southeastern part of the country, the summers feel like you're wrapped in a wet blanket with all that humidity. Here it's much drier—but still hot, all right!"

"The first thing we need to do is get acquainted with the land," Papa said. He tucked his white cowboy hat on his head and ushered Mimi and the kids to the rental car waiting by the airplane hangar. Papa had specially requested a jeep with huge off-road tires, big metal roll bars on the roof, and spotlights for exploring at night. Its shiny red paint gleamed in the bright sun.

"So how do you like our ride?" he asked Mimi.

She smiled and kissed his cheek. "You know it's my favorite color! And as long as it has air conditioning, I'm good to go!"

"It's awesome!" Evan exclaimed.

"You'll soon see lots of things are a bit different out here in the Wild West," Papa announced.

Mimi and Papa lived in Palmetto Bluffs, South Carolina, where the landscape was lush and old oak trees dripped with Spanish moss. Their Lowcountry home was close to the Atlantic Ocean—a far cry from the landlocked city of Tucson.

"I love how you can see for miles and miles here," Avery observed.

"Just wait until you see the sunsets," Mimi said. "They are magnificent!"

Papa laughed. "Like Dorothy said in *The Wizard of Oz*, we're not in 'South Carolina' anymore!"

2

STICKY STICK-UP

The kids watched the bustling city landscape slowly turn into desert rock and sand as they drove southwest of Tucson.

"Don't they have any pine trees here?" Ella asked.

"Tucson may not have pine trees," Mimi said, "but they've got something we don't have back home—cacti!"

"Cat ties?" Evan asked from the back seat. "No way! Cats wear ties in Arizona?"

"Not *cat ties*, Evan," Avery explained with a giggle. "Cacti." She grabbed her iPhone, pulled up a search engine, and quickly found a picture of a saguaro cactus to show her brother.

Its tall **cylindrical** center served as the base for several thick branches. Some branches shot straight up toward the sky while others stuck out sideways and then folded up. Sharp spines grew in neat rows up and down the plant.

Mimi peeked over Avery's shoulder. "There are lots of different types of cacti," she said, "but this saguaro cactus is the most recognizable. It only grows in southern Arizona and western Sonora, Mexico. And just remember, it's pronounced *suh-wah-ro*."

"I wouldn't want to get too close to one of those things!" Evan said.

"Why?" Avery smirked. "Scared it might stick ya?" She grabbed the soft skin of Evan's forearm and squeezed it quickly between her fingers.

"Ouch! She pinched me!" he yelled.

"All right now, young'uns," Papa drawled. "Settle down. We have arrived!" The kids peered out the windows to see a small, tan stucco building shaded by an overhang of orange-brown tiles.

"That house looks like pictures of homes I've seen in Mexico!" Ella said.

"Well, technically, that's not a house," Mimi said. "It's a visitor's center. We're actually at Catalina State Park!"

"Yep," Papa added. "We're going to hike the Nature Trail and stretch our legs a bit. These old doggies are stiff from that long flight." As the kids piled out of the jeep and headed toward the Nature Trail, Avery showed Ella her iPhone.

"You're not too far off about houses here looking like we're in Mexico," Avery said. "Look how close we are to the Mexican border." Ella used her thumb and pointer finger to zoom in on the state of Arizona on a colorful U.S. map.

"Wow!" she said. "Tucson is just north of the border between the United States and Mexico!"

"Stick 'em up!" Evan yelled. Avery and Ella looked up quickly from the iPhone, expecting to see their little brother in some sort of trouble already. Instead, he pointed his finger at a tall cactus. "This here's my territory, and I won't have none of you horse thieves runnin' around," he drawled in his best cowboy accent.

"Umm, Evan," Avery said. "You know you're talking to a cactus, right?"

Evan rolled his blue eyes dramatically at his big sister. "What do you think I am? Crazy?"

"Well—" Avery said.

"That cactus looks like an outlaw with his hands in the air!" Evan interrupted Avery. "Don't you see it?"

Two thick branches poked out of each side of the towering cactus, right where a very tall man's arms might be.

"It does look like a stick figure of somebody surrendering to the sheriff!" Ella admitted, giggling.

"Here," said Mimi, "you can read about the saguaro cacti here." She pointed to a marker along the trail.

"Oh yeah," Avery said. "Now I remember! We learned about these in science! They have roots just a few inches below the ground that soak up water whenever it rains. The cactus stores the water inside for a long time so it has enough to live off of in desert droughts. The spines on the outside are its way of protecting the stored water from thirsty animals."

Ella shielded Avery's smart phone with her hand to see the National Park Service fact sheet she'd pulled up on the Internet. "It says here that a saguaro cactus can live 150-175 years and can be as tall as 50 feet!"

"I'm about four feet tall. That means..." Evan bit his bottom lip and stared up at the sky. Avery recognized his look of concentration.

"Here, use my calculator app." Avery took her phone from Ella and handed it to Evan. Evan typed in 50 and divided it by 4. "That means a cactus could be as tall as twelve and a half of me stacked on top of myself!" he announced.

"That sounds terrifying! Twelve Evans...plus a half-Evan!" Avery faked a shiver and elbowed her brother gently in his chest.

"Hey!" Ella whispered urgently. "Look at that!" Her finger trembled as she pointed at another saguaro cactus just a few feet away from where Mimi stood reading a trail marker. Eight brown, hairy legs moved like tentacles along the dusty turf at the base of the cactus.

It was crawling right toward Mimi!

The saguaro cactus is a
symbol of the American West.

3

CAC-TUSHED

"MIMI!" the kids yelled in unison. Startled, Mimi looked up from the marker she was reading about the Sonoran Desert **ecosystem** to see her grandchildren pointing frantically at her feet.

"Mimi! Move!" Avery yelled. Mimi scurried toward the kids just in time for the giant spider to retreat to a new hiding place under a scraggly green bush.

"What in the world is the problem?" Mimi asked. "Is someone hurt?"

"No, Mimi, we're fine. It was a—" Avery was interrupted by Evan's stuttering.

"I-i-it's moving under that bush!" Evan pointed to two legs sticking out from beneath the bush. The legs slowly kicked in the air like an eerie greeting. "It's some sort of spider monster! We better get out of here fast!"

"It's not a monster, Evan," Mimi said calmly. "It's a tarantula."

"A TARANTULA!" Evan squealed. He scrambled away from the bush to the other side of the trail.

"You best watch where you're going," Papa warned, but it was too late.

"AAHHH!" Evan screamed. "It got me!"

"Evan!" Avery said. "What's wrong?" She ran to her brother. He was crumpled on his hands and knees next to a round cactus, close to the ground and shaped like a barrel. He held his bottom and **winced**.

"Save yourself, Avery. I've been bit. There must be tarantulas all over the place. I can feel the poison running through my body." Evan started to cough. "Tell Mom I love her."

"Evan, you're not dying! Where does it hurt?" Avery asked. Evan pointed to his bottom.

"I can see a light," Evan murmured, reaching his hand toward the sky in front of him.

Ella calmly walked toward her brother and sister, holding Avery's iPhone. "That light must be the desert sun, because a tarantula bite won't kill you." she said. She scrolled through an Internet article about tarantulas. "It says here that a tarantula bite only stings humans like a bee sting. It can't kill you unless you're allergic to them."

"Ella's right," Avery said. "You are going to be just fine, especially because your ouchie was not caused by a tarantula!" Avery grabbed a long skinny thorn sticking through Evan's shorts and pulled hard.

"OWWWW!" Evan screeched.

"You got bit by a cactus!" Avery announced. "This a cactus spine. It looks kind of like a long thorn."

Evan smiled weakly, embarrassed. "I knew I'd be all right."

"Ha ha, Evan, you just got cac-tushed!" Ella teased. She pulled out the digital camera she had stuffed in her shorts pocket and snapped a photo of the barrel cactus behind her brother. "I don't want to forget this!"

"Now," Mimi said, "since everyone's OK, we need to get to the University of Arizona campus. I'm supposed to meet Professor Clark in an hour." Papa hurried Mimi and the kids back to the parking lot. The kids' eyes were glued to the ground, searching for any sign of spiders. When they got to the jeep, Evan slid slowly onto the seat on his sore bottom.

"I'm glad that's over," Evan said. "I can't say I'm crazy about the bugs and insects here in Arizona!"

"Spiders aren't actually insects," Avery said. "They're in a group called arachnids, along with scorpions and ticks."

"Yuck," Evan said. "That group sounds pretty bad, too!" He shivered at the thought of scorpions and spiders anywhere around him.

"In school this year, we learned some easy ways to tell insects and arachnids apart," Avery announced. "Insects use antennae to feel, and arachnids use hairs on their legs to feel. Insects have six legs, and arachnids have eight legs. Insects have three sections on their body, and arachnids only have two."

"That's right! They have the abdomen and the **cephalothorax**," Ella added. She showed Evan the webpage she pulled up on the iPhone.

"Self-a-lo-wax? What is that?" Evan asked. "Whatever—I guess I'm not crazy about the *arachnids* here in Arizona!"

"Don't be so sure about that," Mimi remarked, leaning over the front seat. "Bugs and creatures like arachnids are pretty amazing! Professor Clark is going to teach me everything he knows about Arizona bugs. I know you'll learn a lot, too!"

Evan grunted and rubbed his sore spot. He wasn't sure he wanted to know one more thing about Arizona's creepy crawlies!

4

AGENT 008-LEGS

The University of Arizona campus sprawled across the desert landscape. Students with earbuds jammed in their ears crowded the sidewalks and streets, trying to get to their next class on time. Signs pointed students and visitors to buildings specifically designated for mathematics, history, business, science, and other subjects.

Papa pulled up the jeep near a salmon-colored brick building with gleaming white columns known as the Forbes Building. Mimi and the kids hopped out of the car while Papa drove to find a parking space. Inside the glass doors, classrooms and small offices lined long hallways. The group took the elevator to the entomology department.

A smiling man with short dark hair parted and brushed to the side greeted them as the elevator opened. He wore faded jeans and a brown corduroy suit coat with round beige patches at the elbows.

"Welcome to the University of Arizona!" he announced. "I've been looking forward to meeting Roo's favorite mystery author!"

"Hello, Professor Clark!" Mimi said. "And I'm excited to learn all about Arizona crawling critters from a world-class expert! I hope you don't mind; I brought my grandchildren with me. This is Avery, Ella, and Evan." The kids waved shyly at the professor.

"Not at all," Professor Clark replied. "In fact, my daughter Roo is waiting in my office." He led Mimi and the kids down the hall to his crowded office. Inside, a tall window showered light on a wide wooden desk strewn with papers, and bookshelves stuffed with books.

One shelf in particular caught Evan's eye. It wasn't filled with books, but with dozens of square, see-through cases displaying beetles, spiders, and scorpions. *Why would you want to look at them every day?* he thought.

A freckle-faced girl around Ella's age sat cross-legged in the corner. Her chestnut hair was French braided into two pigtails that ended just below her shoulders. She wore denim shorts and a bright aqua shirt with a smiling purple and green cartoon spider on the front. Evan shook his head. *She likes these bugs and spiders, too!*

"Roo, meet Carole Marsh," Professor Clark said. Roo's sparkling brown eyes lit up. She hurried over to Mimi to shake her hand.

"I love your mystery books!" she said. "I read every one I can get my hands on! I even read them twice sometimes!"

"Thank you, honey," Mimi said, beaming. "I love meeting my fans! And here are my grandkids—Avery, Ella, and Evan—to meet you, too." Avery and Ella smiled and waved.

"Why would you want *that* on your shirt?" Evan blurted out. He pointed at the cartoon spider.

"Oh, don't mind him," Ella said. "He had a run-in with a cactus earlier, by way of a tarantula!"

Roo looked puzzled, then shrugged her shoulders. "Come with me," she offered, and led the kids to a nearby study room so Mimi and Professor Clark could talk. The study room sat on the corner of the building with massive windows overlooking the clean, manicured campus.

"Actually," Roo said as she quietly shut the door behind them, "I love spiders. And tarantulas are my absolute favorite!"

Evan stared at Roo with wide eyes and an open mouth. "How could *anyone* love spiders?"

"I grew up around them," Roo said. "My dad works with all kinds of insects and arachnids. They are actually pretty cool when you learn about them. So what kind of tarantula did you see?"

"One about this big," Evan described. He held his bony arms out as wide as he could stretch. "And it had hair all over it!"

Ella shook her head. "Actually, it was *this* big, and it was dark brown with tiny hairs on its legs," she corrected. She held her thumbs and pointer fingers together to form a circle a few inches across.

"I'll bet you saw an Arizona Desert Tarantula," Roo decided. "They're very common around here." She looked at Evan. "But they aren't quite *that* big. They usually only grow to about 13 centimeters long."

"Centimeters?" Ella asked.

"My dad uses the **metric system** in his studies, so he taught it to me," Roo said. "One centimeter is 0.39370 inches."

Avery quickly brought up the calculator app on her phone. "That means we could multiply that number, 0.39370, by 13 to get the average size of the tarantula in inches." She quickly typed in the numbers.

"The answer is 5.11," Avery read off the calculator. "So, the average length of an Arizona Desert Tarantula is about 5 inches. Your dad must use a lot of STEM in his work."

"You mean STEM, which stands for Science, Technology, Engineering, and Math?" Roo asked. "We use STEM in school a lot, and yep, my dad uses it at work every day!"

As the kids talked, Ella looked up tarantulas on the iPhone. "Hey Roo, it says here that the Mexican red-kneed tarantula is the most commonly used tarantula in movies and TV shows because it is so recognizable. What do they look like?"

"Oooh, they are just the coolest!" Roo exclaimed. Her eyes lit up as she described the spider. "They have a mostly brown body, and their legs look kind of brown-and-white striped with orange-red marks near the top of their legs. I guess you could call that their knees!"

"Remind me not to see a movie starring Agent 008-Legs," Evan mumbled.

Roo laughed. "You might like them if you got a good look at one." She suddenly raised her eyebrows and grinned. "C'mon, I want to show you guys something!" She grabbed Evan's hand and yanked him down the hall toward the elevator. Avery and Ella scurried after them.

When they heard the loud "DING" for the fourth floor, Roo smiled. "Here we are, at the University of Arizona Insect Collection!"

She led the kids down a hall and into a massive room. Hundreds of bugs covered the walls! Evan and Ella could not believe what they were seeing. A horrified shiver shook Avery's spine from top to bottom!

5

INSECT INSPECTION

Avery breathed a sigh of relief when she noticed none of the bugs were moving. They were neatly displayed in glass cases. Below each case was a plaque nailed to the wall bearing a description of the insect.

One of the workers in the room smiled at Roo and nodded her permission to give the kids a tour. The first collection was a stunning display of delicate butterflies. Each had their wings spread wide to showcase the **intricate**, multicolored designs. A butterfly with burnt orange and ebony wings stood out to Avery. Its elaborate wing design looked like a gorgeous painting.

"I love this monarch butterfly!" Avery gushed. "I cannot believe how beautiful it is up close."

"I never really thought of butterflies as insects before," Evan said.

"They fit the insect description," Ella said. "They have antennae, six legs, and three sections to their bodies."

"Well, maybe I do like *some* insects, then," Evan admitted.

Beetles adorned the next wall. Some boasted shiny green shells. Others had big, spiky horns **protruding** from their heads.

"This one's absolutely huge!" Evan shouted, pointing to a beetle the size of his hand. Two horns that looked like they formed the letter C jutted from its head.

Avery gasped and shivered again. "I think I feel a nightmare coming tonight," she mumbled.

"Oh, that's the Hercules beetle," Roo said. "It's the largest in the United States."

"The beetles all look like they're wearing armor," Evan said. He craned his neck to scan the wall from top to bottom.

"That's their exoskeleton," Ella informed her brother. "We learned about that in science class, too. It's the hard outer layer on animals like beetles. It's like their skeleton is worn on the outside of their bodies instead of the inside. It makes them strong and protects them from predators."

"Oh, so that's why you hear a CRRRUUNCH when you squish a beetle," Evan said. He stomped his foot on the floor and turned it around in a grinding motion. Avery shot him a disapproving look. He grinned at his sister as they headed toward a sign saying "Arachnids." It hung over displays of scorpions and spiders.

"I think I'll wait over by the butterflies," Evan said. He spun around toward the entrance of the Insect Collection.

"Oh, no, you don't!" Ella grabbed the shoulder of Evan's blue t-shirt and pulled him back around. "We're just getting to the best part!"

Evan glared at Ella while Roo led them past an eerie array of scorpions on the way to the spiders. Some spiders were as tiny as the tip of a sewing needle. Others sported bright red or yellow stripes down their back. Every one of them made Evan's skin crawl. Avery felt a little queasy, but she made sure not to let her little brother know it.

Finally, at the end of the seemingly endless display of spiders, Roo pointed out the largest, hairiest of all.

"Here it is, the Mexican red-kneed tarantula!" Roo said proudly. The kids slowly leaned in to take a closer look at the display. Tiny hairs like fur stuck out from the spider's legs and body. Where the legs bent at the joint was a stripe of bright orange and red.

The tarantula's thick body was separated into two round parts. "See, that's the abdomen and the cephalothorax," Avery pointed out. The body was beige-brown with a black square marking on top. Next to the spider, a display showed the bottom of a Mexican red-kneed tarantula where two sharp fangs poked out from the body.

"All the better to eat you with," Evan muttered. "This is giving me the creeps and goosebumps all at once!" He held out his arm covered in tiny, prickly bumps for his sisters to see.

"There's really nothing to be afraid of," Roo said. "They aren't vampires! Tarantulas don't usually bite people unless they are **provoked**. But if one did bite you, you'd only feel a sting for a little while."

"So what do they eat?" Avery asked.

"They eat other insects and sometimes baby mice or birds," Roo said. "It's actually kind of cool. They bite their prey and inject them with venom that helps them digest the prey's insides. Then the tarantulas suck up the guts through their fangs and leave a little **carcass** of dried-up insect when they're done."

"Ewwww!" the kids shouted.

"What's wrong with that?" Roo said. "I think it's awesome! We all have to eat; that's just how tarantulas gobble up their dinner."

"I vant to suck your blooood," Evan teased Ella in a vampire voice as they followed Roo toward the caterpillars.

Avery lingered at the tarantula display to read more kind-of-disgusting, but kind-of-cool facts. She noticed a piece of paper on the floor tucked up against the wall. She leaned down to pick it up and realized it was a folded note.

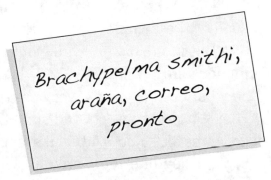

Brachypelma smithi, araña, correo, pronto

Avery couldn't understand any of the words. She wondered what the note meant and who it was meant for. A sense of urgency rose within her. She thought, *I need to find out what those words mean!*

6

CRITTERS AND
A CLUE

Avery stuffed the letter into the pocket of her capri jeans and decided to keep it to herself—for now, anyway. She joined the other kids who had moved on to a section filled with wasps. Their bodies were displayed in neat little rows in glass cases on the wall.

"Look at this one!" Evan said. He pointed to a small black wasp with reddish orange wings.

Ella snuck up behind her brother and pinched his arm. "BZZZZ!"

Evan jumped. "That's not funny!" he cried. "I thought that thing was alive!"

Ella giggled. Evan straightened his shoulders. "As I was saying," he remarked, glaring at his sister, "this wasp is called a Tarantula Hawk."

"That's funny," Ella said. "It doesn't look like a tarantula or a hawk."

"This little wasp is actually a powerful predator of the tarantula," Roo said. "That's where it gets its name. It lays eggs on the tarantula's back and when the eggs hatch, the babies eat the spider alive!"

"Oh my gosh!" Evan grimaced. "Why does everything about tarantulas have to be so gross?"

"I'm surprised a tarantula could be hurt by such a little wasp," Avery added. "It seems like the tarantula wouldn't have too many predators. It's so big and hairy and scary looking!"

"That's just the circle of life in our ecosystem," Roo explained. "Everything has a predator. It's actually a good thing. Tarantulas keep the number of bugs and critters under control, and this little wasp helps keep the number of tarantulas under control. That way, nothing **overpopulates** the environment.

"But," she continued, "wasps aren't the tarantula's only predator. One of their biggest dangers is us."

"Nope, uh uh, they don't have to worry about me," Evan said, shaking his blond head. "I won't get anywhere close to one!"

"Some people kill tarantulas just because they look scary," Roo explained. "They use tarantula traps to catch and kill them."

Avery quickly looked up "tarantula traps" on her phone.

"Look at this!" she said. "You can build a trap with just an empty soup can and some leaves."

"That's right," Roo agreed. "Around here, people bury the empty soup can in the ground, cover the top with leaves, and wait for the tarantula to crawl over the top and fall in. People don't want them crawling around their backyards."

"I don't blame them!" Avery said. Evan nodded in agreement.

"I know, but I always hope that instead of killing them, people will move trapped tarantulas to a safe environment," Roo said.

"Some people even catch tarantulas and smuggle them to other countries illegally."

"Why would they do that?" Avery asked.

"Tarantulas make really good pets!" Roo explained.

Evan stared at her in disbelief. "We are still talking about the giant, hairy spider with two sharp fangs, right?" he asked.

"Yes, I am!" Roo replied. "They can live up to 30 years, they are usually **docile**, and they are very easy to take care of. Some people will pay a lot of money for them," Roo said.

"And some people are crazy, too," Evan declared.

Avery smiled. "But you can't play fetch or snuggle with a tarantula," she objected. Evan pictured a tarantula playing fetch with a tiny tennis ball and started giggling.

While the kids talked, Ella wandered across the room back to the butterfly exhibit. She was studying a butterfly with bright blue and black wings when she noticed movement out of the corner of her eye. She slowly turned toward the arachnid display across the room and saw a tall man in a tailored black suit with a white shirt and black tie. A gray **fedora** was perched on his head. It had a black ribbon around the center and a small brown feather tucked under it.

The man studied the Mexican red-kneed tarantula display. Suddenly, he noticed Ella watching him, and scowled at her. She hurried back to join to the others, her heart thumping.

"Don't look now," she whispered to Avery, "but we're not the only ones interested in tarantulas!"

Avery peeked toward the spider display just in time to see the man in black kneeling in front of the information plaque and feeling the ground with his hand.

Uh oh! she thought. *Is he looking for that note—the one tucked away in my pocket?*

7

SPIDER SPAGHETTI

Roo convinced her father to invite Mimi, Papa, and the kids over to their house for dinner that night. Professor Clark thought it would be a great opportunity to continue his conversation with Mimi. Roo was excited to spend more time with her new friends and show them a surprise!

A cheerful, red-headed woman in a blue-and-white striped apron met the family at the door. "Hi, I'm Sarah Clark," she said, "Roo's mom. I hope you like spaghetti and meatballs!"

Evan's eyes lit up. "I sure do!" he said. "I'm so hungry, I could eat an entire pot of spaghetti on my own!" He patted his growling stomach.

Sarah smiled. "Good!" she said. "Dinner's almost ready. Roo is upstairs if you want to play for a little while," she offered. The kids bounded up the wooden staircase while Mimi and Papa talked with Sarah and Professor Clark in the kitchen.

At the end of the hall, the kids spotted a purple sign that said "Roo" in letters decorated with ladybugs, caterpillars, and smiling spiders. Through the cracked-open door, they could see Roo playing with something on her bedroom floor.

"Hi, Roo!" Avery said. "I love your room!" Bright purple paint covered the walls, contrasting with a white bunk bed and dresser. Toys were strewn across the floor. In the middle of them sat a square plastic box with a pink lid.

"Hi!" Roo said with a big smile. "I'm so glad you could come over!"

"Do you have any cool toys for boys in here?" Evan asked. He scanned the room and rolled his eyes. Stuffed animals, princess dress-up clothes, and bottles of nail polish dotted the carpeted floor.

"I've got just the thing!" Roo said. "Why don't you guys come over here and sit down?" She directed them to sit around the plastic box.

"So?" Evan said. "Where are your cool toys?"

"Well, technically, this is not a toy," Roo replied. "But it is very cool!" She held the box close to her eye and peeked in the side of it. "Can you see it?"

"Is this a joke?" Evan said. He folded his arms in front of his chest. "No one likes playing with rocks, Roo."

"Let's look closer," Ella urged. Now she was staring into the clear plastic box, too.

"I see it!" Avery blurted out. "Oh my goodness, Roo, is that yours?"

"What? I don't see anything!" Evan complained. Roo tapped the side of the box lightly with her fingernail. What looked like a brown rock stretched out eight furry legs and began to crawl slowly across the bottom of the box.

Evan clambered to his feet. "Is that what I think it is?"

"This is Fluffy, my pet tarantula," Roo said. She pursed her lips together and talked in a baby voice to the giant spider. "Aren't you a cute little girl!"

"Fluffy?" Avery said. "Seriously? That's a funny name for a spider."

"My dad bought her for me on my sixth birthday," Roo said. "That was a few years ago."

"If tarantulas can live up to 30 years, then Fluffy could stick around until you're like, almost 40!" Evan did the math quickly in his head and shuddered. "That's just *toooo* long!"

"So that's how you know so much about tarantulas," Ella observed.

"Yep! Fluffy is a Mexican red-kneed tarantula," Roo said. "See the red markings on her legs?" Roo pointed out eight bright red lines. "I wanted to surprise you with her in person!"

"You definitely surprised me!" Evan said. "I can't believe you have one of these in your bedroom!"

"Do you guys want to hold her?" Roo popped the edge of the pink plastic lid off the box. Avery realized the box was actually a small, portable animal cage with slots in the lid and a handle.

"NO!" Avery and Evan yelled, stepping back quickly.

"DO NOT take that spider out!" Evan ordered.

"She won't hurt you, I promise," Roo said. "How about you, Ella?"

Ella eyed the spider curiously. "Umm, maybe next time."

"Chicken!" Evan taunted.

"Like you have any room to talk!" Ella said. Roo handed Ella the plastic cage so she could see Fluffy up close, but still safely inside.

"Did you catch this in a tarantula trap like you told us about?" Avery asked.

"No, my father knows a man who sells tarantulas approved by the CITES treaty," Roo replied.

"CITES?" Ella asked.

"That's short for the Convention on International Trade in Endangered Species of Wild Fauna and Flora," Roo recited.

"That's a lot of words!" Evan said. "Can you translate that, please?"

"The CITES treaty protects animals like the Mexican red-kneed tarantula from being illegally smuggled across countries," Roo explained. "It's meant to protect species that are endangered or at risk of disappearing from their natural habitat. My dad had to make sure the seller he bought Fluffy from didn't **import** spiders illegally."

"Does Fluffy live in this little cage all the time?" Avery asked. The enclosure wasn't much bigger than the spider creeping slowly inside it.

"Oh no," Roo laughed. "That's her real home." Roo pointed to a large glass tank Avery hadn't noticed before. It nestled under one of Roo's windows. The tank contained a bowl of water, plus soil and a few rocks on the bottom. In one of the corners, a terra cotta pot was turned on its side and buried in dirt to resemble a cave with a small opening.

"My mom and I are cleaning the cricket guts out of her cage, so she gets to stay in this spidey-hotel," Roo said. She set the cage back on the floor.

"Are you sure that lid's on tight enough?" Evan asked. He eyed Fluffy from a safe distance.

"Yes, but one time Fluffy did escape," Roo said, with a mischievous look in her eyes. "We didn't find her for three days."

"Where was she?" Ella asked.

"Mom found her in the big pasta pot under the sink," Roo replied. "We still don't know how she got in there!"

"Suddenly I don't feel so hungry anymore," Evan said with a moan. Ella laughed at her little brother.

"I sort of have a surprise of my own," Avery blurted out. "Although I don't know if it's a good one."

"Do you mean the man in black we saw at the insect collection?" Ella asked. "He was looking at the arachnid display and gave me a mean look!"

"I wouldn't have thought much about it," Avery said, "except that I saw him kneel down and search the floor around the tarantula display. That's where I found this just a few minutes before he came in." Avery pulled the folded up note out of her pocket.

"Do you think this might be a real life mystery?" Roo asked. An excited smile spread across her face.

"I don't know," Avery said. "But we need to be careful with this guy. He looked scary!" She unfolded the note and read the strange words aloud to the kids. "I have no idea what any of this means, and I want to find out."

"Sounds like someone was writing gibberish to me," Evan joked.

"Those first words sound like Latin," Ella said. Avery and Evan stared at her.

"How do *you* know that?" Evan asked.

"In science class last year, we learned that **scientific names** are written in Latin," Ella replied. "Maybe we should look up the first two words and see if they're the name of something."

Roo offered Ella her pink laptop. Ella carefully typed *Brachypelma smithi* into the search engine.

"Oh, wow!" Avery cried, peering over Ella's shoulder. Pictures of tarantulas had popped up under the "Images" link. "Mexican Red-Kneed Tarantula" was written in big blue letters across the top of the page.

"The man in black was researching Mexican red-kneed tarantulas just like we are!" Avery said. She suspected it wasn't a coincidence.

"But what does it all mean?" Roo asked.

"Maybe he wants us to stay away from tarantulas," Evan suggested. "I'd be OK with a mystery like that!"

Later that night, Avery quietly unfolded the clue in their dark hotel room. She used the flashlight app on her phone to illuminate the message and read the words over and over again.

She didn't know exactly what the note meant, but she didn't think it had been written for them. *Or had it been?*

Ella searches for the meaning of
words in the clue.

8

HOLD YOUR HORSES

The next morning, Papa took the kids to Roo's favorite horseback riding spot while Professor Clark and Mimi continued their research at the university.

"There's nothing like riding horses along a desert trail to experience the real Wild West!" Roo said.

Four coffee-colored horses stood patiently tied to posts in front of their freshly painted, rust-red stable. Openings in the stable walls revealed even more horses resting in their stalls. Some stuck their heads out of the openings to feel the warm morning sun.

Next to the horses outside the stable, a small, gray-and-white spotted horse drank water from a **trough**. A pretty woman with short blonde hair held back with a bright red bandana brushed the mane of the horse next to him. She smiled broadly when she heard Papa and the kids walk up.

"I've been expecting you guys," she said. "I'm Susie, and I'll be your tour guide this morning. Let's get you saddled up!"

The scent of hay and pungent horse manure greeted the kids as soon as they walked up. Evan pinched his nose shut. "Pee-YOO!" he exclaimed.

Susie cocked her head and smiled at Evan. "That's just the smell of the stable environment!" she said. "You'll get used to it."

Susie helped Papa and the girls mount the brown horses first. Then she turned her attention to Evan. "Your turn, little man," she said, leading him to the spotted horse. "This is Pronto. He's just the right fit for you."

Evan stared suspiciously at the spotted horse. "Sort of an ugly duckling, isn't he?"

"Oh, no! I think his spots are beautiful," Susie replied. She smoothed her hand over Pronto's white mane and helped Evan into the saddle. As soon as Evan was settled, Pronto shook his head and blew air through his nose in a loud "Pfoooofffff!"

"Whoa! Good boy, Pronto," Evan said, patting his neck. "I take it back. You're very handsome. I didn't mean to offend you." Pronto pawed the ground with his right hoof as if in response to Evan's apology. He shook his head quickly from side-to-side and yanked the reins out of Evan's hands.

"Hey, stop that," Evan complained.

"I'll stay near you," Susie reassured Evan. "Pronto seems a little frisky today."

Avery poked Roo in the arm. "I knew that sounded familiar," she whispered.

"What?" Roo asked.

"Pronto, the name of Evan's horse," Avery said. "It's one of the words in the clue!"

"Do you think the clue's about the horse?" Roo asked.

"Not exactly," Avery said. She suspected the word might have another meaning she didn't know yet.

"YAH!" Susie yelled. She perched confidently on top of a shiny black horse with a thick mane. She kicked her boots gently back and forth, coaxing him to move forward.

"This is my horse, Lightning," Susie said. "Y'all follow me!" On cue, all five horses fell into step behind Susie and Lightning. Susie led them down a dusty trail lined with cacti and desert shrubs. The bright blue sky stretched before them like an ocean touching the tip of the desert sand. Dust spiraled in a cloud around the horses' hooves as they click-clacked along the winding trail.

"You'll see the beautiful environment of the Sonoran Desert all around you," Susie explained. "But be on the watch for local critters. We've been known to spot a rattlesnake or two on this trail!"

"Why is the horse Evan is riding named Pronto?" Avery asked unexpectedly.

Susie turned and smiled. "It's a bit of a joke," she explained. "That word means 'quick' in Spanish. He's actually kind of slow-moving, so we nicknamed him the opposite!"

WHEEE!! WHEEE!! Suddenly, Pronto screeched and reared up halfway into the air. "WHOOOOAAA!" cried Evan. He clutched the reins, trying desperately to hang onto the terrified horse.

Susie spied a diamond-patterned rattlesnake slinking off the trail. "Hang on, Evan!" Susie shouted. "I'm coming!"

But Pronto was not in the mood to wait. He darted down the trail, determined to escape from the reptile that had terrified him. Evan wrapped his arms around Pronto's neck, his blond head thumping up and down as the horse bolted.

A group of riders ahead of Evan realized what was happening and formed a **barricade** to block Pronto. As the horse slowed down, a rider in a black cowboy hat grabbed the reins. "Whooaaaa, little guy," the rider said, doing his best to soothe Pronto's nerves. "Everything's all right now. Just calm down."

Susie and Papa arrived close behind. "Evan!" Papa shouted. "Are you OK?"

Evan's face was still buried in Pronto's thick mane. "Is it over?" he asked.

Papa lifted Evan off his horse and held him in a big bear hug. "You're safe now," he said. He set Evan snugly in the front of his saddle. "You'll be riding with me now!"

Evan nodded. "I like that idea, Papa!"

Susie thanked the riders for their help and led Pronto next to Lightning back down the trail. Papa and Evan followed them. Once they joined the girls, Avery, Ella, and Roo peppered Evan with questions. "Are you OK?" "Were you scared?" "Did you see the snake?" "I guess that Pronto was pretty quick, huh?"

Once she knew her brother was safe, Avery's mind wandered back to the clue. *Spanish—I should have known that, she thought.* She wanted to look up the rest of the words from the clue, but that would have to wait. *Now, the short desert trail seemed a million miles long.*

9

HOME, SWEET TARANTULA HOME

"Look!" Roo shouted. She pointed toward the right side of the trail as the horses slowly sauntered along. The sandy specks of dirt on the ground seemed to sparkle in the morning sunshine that was getting hotter and hotter. "I think that's a tarantula's burrow!"

The kids spied a small, perfectly round hole in the sand surrounded by a net of thick, silky web.

"You're right," Susie said. "That's probably home to an Arizona Desert Tarantula."

"Have your horses ever stepped on one?" Ella asked.

Susie shook her head. "No," she replied. "Believe it or not, tarantulas keep to themselves. The only time they wander from their burrows is during mating season, and that's only the males. The females spend most of their time in their burrows."

"My dad says that a tarantula can live in the same burrow its whole life," Roo added.

"They must be homebodies like me," Papa joked. "What I wouldn't give for a nap in my recliner right about now." He let out a huge yawn. "And an ice-cold glass of sweet tea!"

"Then I guess it's a good thing we're almost finished!" Susie said. She led the horses around a wide curve back to the stable where they started. She swung her leg over Lightning's broad back and stepped out of the saddle.

"You guys are naturals!" she said to the girls. She helped them **dismount** their horses. "And Evan, you did a great job staying on Pronto. I'm just so sorry about that and thankful you are all right. You are one brave kid!"

Papa lifted Evan out of their shared saddle. Evan groaned when he stood up straight. He ambled toward the girls with his legs spread apart like he was bowlegged.

"I think I'm going to be sore," he said. He held the inside of his thighs. "I guess I was hanging on with my legs and my arms! I didn't even know I had muscles there to get sore!" Ella and Roo giggled.

Susie invited Papa into her office to cool off while the kids explored the stable. "Just don't stand behind the horses—they can kick!" Susie warned.

Avery huddled the kids together as soon as Papa rounded the corner of the stable toward the office. She was anxious to share her new discovery.

"It's Spanish!" she said. She unfolded the note from her pocket. "I should have caught it earlier. *Pronto* means 'quick' in Spanish." She read the note again to the group.

"Quick? He was quick all right!" Evan said.

"No, Evan," Avery said. "Not your horse, the clue!"

Avery grabbed her iPhone out of the small tote bag she'd left on a big silver hook inside the stable.

"We have to look up these other words," she said. "I have a feeling they might be Spanish, too!"

Avery quickly typed in *araña* and *correo* in her translator app. "Spider" and "mail" showed up instantly.

"Now we know what the clue says!" Ella cried.

"Mexican red-kneed tarantula, spider, mail, quick," Roo recited.

"Don't get too excited," Avery said. "We know what it says, but we still don't know what it means."

"Why is it written in Spanish?" Ella asked. "Do you think the man in black is from Mexico?"

"It's hard to say," Avery replied. "We don't know anything about him."

"Lots of people around here are **bilingual**," Roo added. "We are so close to the Mexican border that many people speak Spanish as a second or even first language.

I know some Spanish myself, but I didn't recognize those words in the note."

"One thing I feel sure of is that this note wasn't written for us," Avery said. "It was left for someone else to find but we got to it first."

"It seems like all the words go together except for mail," Roo remarked. "Spider and Mexican red-kneed tarantula make sense together. And tarantulas can be quick. But mail? I don't see how it fits."

"Hey guys!" Evan interrupted the girls' concentration. "There's something over here." Evan knelt down beside a small hole in the ground near the edge of the stable. The dirt around the hole looked freshly dug. Something shiny glimmered in the sun.

"Evan! I think that's a tarantula burrow," Avery shouted.

"WHAAAT?!" Evan scampered backwards with his hands behind him. He looked like a crab quickly retreating.

"It looks just like the one we saw on the trail!" Avery added.

Ella bravely walked toward the burrow and squatted beside it. She ran her fingers around the edge of the hole.

"Ella..." Avery warned her sister.

"This isn't a tarantula burrow," Ella said confidently. "See, there's no webbing on the outside." Ella plunged her hand deep into the black hole. Avery gasped.

"AHHHH!" Ella screeched.

Avery grabbed her sister by the shoulders. "Ella! Ella! Are you OK?" Avery frantically yanked her sister away from the hole.

"Hahahaha! I got you!" Ella said, giggling. "I'm perfectly fine!"

"You scared me to death!" Avery said.

"Well, you won't be able to stay mad at me for long. Look!" Ella held up her hand. Between her fingers was a black piece of construction paper folded into a tiny square.

"It isn't a tarantula burrow," Ella explained. "It's a tarantula trap! The shiny thing we saw was the edge of the soup can buried in the ground. This was inside it!"

Avery snatched the paper out of Ella's hand and unfolded it. Silver ink scrawled a **menacing** message on the black paper:

Soft as silk, sticky sweet, once it's caught, it cannot leave.

"Another clue!" Roo said.

"But what in the world does it mean?" Ella asked, even though she knew no one had the answer.

"One thing's for sure," Avery said. "That tarantula trap was freshly buried. Whocvcr left that clue was just here!" Goosebumps prickled on Avery's arm. *Is the man in black following us?*

Papa's deep voice snapped Avery out of her thoughts. "You all ready to head 'em up and move 'em out?" he asked. He handed a bottle of ice-cold water to each child.

Avery quickly stuffed the clue into her bag and followed the others to the jeep. As they drove back to the university to pick up Mimi for lunch, Avery couldn't stop thinking about the clue. This one was so different from the last one. Still, some of the words stuck out to her. *She couldn't shake the feeling that a hidden message was buried in the clue, like a riddle she couldn't figure out.*

10

BUGGY MCGEE

Papa pulled into the university parking lot right at noon. "Let's sit out here in the shade," Papa said. "I'll text Mimi and tell her we're waiting outside."

A flat strip of lush green grass separated the building from the street. Wispy trees and some tall palms dotted the lawn and provided little spots of shade from the scorching sun. Papa headed toward a couple of brick benches near the trees. He stretched out his legs, cocked his cowboy hat over his eyes, and settled in for a quick power nap.

Ella, Roo, and Avery plopped down on a bench completely covered in shade. Evan followed them, his legs still spread wide. He grabbed the bench behind him and gently lowered himself to sit.

"This must be what getting old feels like," Evan moaned.

"You still look like a spring chicken to me, young man," a voice said. It came from the sidewalk a few feet away.

A short man with a round belly smiled at the kids. He wore khaki shorts, a thin white button-down shirt, and a brown safari hat. He walked toward the kids and took his hat off once he reached the shade, revealing his bald head.

Papa pushed his cowboy hat back and greeted the stranger.

"The name's McGee," the man said. He shook Papa's hand. "Henry McGee."

"You were just talking to my grandson," Papa said. "Evan, meet Henry McGee."

Evan stood quickly and grimaced at the soreness in his legs. He grabbed the man's hand and shook as hard as he could.

"Whoa," Henry remarked. "You've got quite a grip there." Evan puffed out his chest and nodded confidently. Then he slowly lowered himself down onto the bench again.

"You'll have to excuse my little brother," Avery explained. "He had an adventure on a runaway horse today!"

"Ah, I see," Henry said. "So do you kids go to college here?" He winked at Papa.

Roo and Ella giggled at the silly question.

"Of course not!" Roo said. "My dad's a professor here and he's doing research with their grandma this week." Roo nodded toward Avery, Ella, and Evan.

"We're waiting for Mimi so we can go to lunch," Avery added.

"She's late as usual!" Papa joked.

"Interesting," Henry said with a smile. "I thought I might be in the presence of some kid super-geniuses!"

"We *are* pretty smart," Ella said.

"Oh, I don't doubt it," Henry said. "Sadly, I can't say the same about myself. I seem to be lost!"

"Maybe we can help," Papa offered. "This is the Forbes Building."

"I have this GPS thingy here," Henry said, "but it doesn't seem to be working right." He pulled out a small square GPS and clicked a few buttons. A digital woman's voice repeated "Recalculating" over and over again.

Henry looked so confused that Avery reached for his GPS. "I can help you with that," she said. She pressed the button to create a new route. "All we have to do is type in the address of where we are now."

"I know the address here by heart!" Roo said. Avery handed her the GPS and Roo quickly typed it.

"Now we just have to put in address of where you want to go," Avery said.

Henry smiled. "You really are kid-geniuses," he said. "I'm trying to get back to my pet shop in downtown Tucson. I just get confused getting off this campus." Avery handed Henry the GPS and helped him type the address in the "Destination" spot.

"Why did you come here?" Ella asked. "I came to campus to meet an old friend's son for an early lunch," Henry replied. He quickly changed the subject. "So what type of professor is your father?" he asked Roo.

"He's an entomology professor," she said. "He's basically a bug expert."

"Very interesting," Henry said. "Does he ever get live bugs to study?"

"Oh sure. Right now he's studying the emperor scorpion." Roo was always happy to talk about her father's job.

"Scorpions, eh?" Henry said. "Does he study tarantulas? I have a few at my pet shop."

"Those are my favorite!" Roo said. "Yes, he studies all kinds of tarantulas."

"Perfect!" Henry said. "I mean, your father sounds like an interesting guy!"

"Oh, he is!" Roo beamed with pride.

"Say, you kids should come visit my pet shop while you're in town," Henry offered. "You can see some Arizona critters up close and personal!"

"Can we, Papa?" Ella asked. Papa nodded at his granddaughter and smiled. Ella secretly wanted another chance to hold a tarantula. She decided she wouldn't chicken out this time.

"Great!" Henry said. "It's called Henry's Pet Emporium. I'll bet you can find it on those high tech phones there."

Just then, Mimi and Professor Clark walked through the front doors, laughing loudly.

"Well, I'll be seeing you," Henry said. He quickly dashed down the sidewalk to a tiny, two-door blue car.

"Who's up for some Tex Mex?" Mimi asked when she reached the benches.

"Trex mix?" Evan said. He furrowed his brow in confusion. "Don't you mean trail mix, Mimi?"

"No, I mean Tex Mex," Mimi repeated. "It's Mexican food with a little bit of Texas flair. Tucson has some great Tex Mex restaurants."

"You have to try the fresh tortillas," Professor Clark said. "Smear them with a little butter and they taste like dessert!"

"Oh, and make sure you try the jalapeño pepper," Roo said to Evan. She smiled mischievously at Avery and Ella. "You can't leave Tucson without tasting one!"

"I'll eat three!" Evan said. "I'm starving! And Mimi, just wait till you hear what happened to me today!"

11

WEB WATCHERS

After lunch, Mimi and Papa agreed to let the kids spend the night at Roo's house.

"Be ready for a big day at the zoo tomorrow," Papa said.

"Have fun!" Mimi shouted as Papa started the jeep. She waved her red silk scarf out the window. "Now, let's get that air conditioning going! I feel like I'm melting!"

Once Papa's jeep had disappeared down the road, Evan held his hand up to his throat.

"I need a glass of water!" he said to Roo.

"Another one?" Ella teased. "This must be your hundredth glass since lunch."

"Why don't *you* try taking a bite of raw jalapeño!" Evan complained. "It just keeps burning!"

Avery and Ella laughed. "I didn't think you'd actually do it," Roo said.

"Never underestimate Evan!" Avery said.

"It didn't even taste good," Evan whined. Roo led the kids up to her bedroom and ran downstairs to get Evan a drink. She returned with a tall glass of ice-cold milk.

"You don't have water?" Evan asked. He eyed the milk and scrunched up his nose.

"Of course we do, but milk will help the burn go away," Roo said. "It's a scientific fact." Evan chugged the glass, leaving a drippy white milk mustache as evidence.

"It actually does feel better," he said. He plopped into a purple bean bag chair, relieved and relaxed.

"Why milk?" Avery asked.

"It counteracts the capsaicin in the pepper," Roo answered. "I did my science fair project on it last year. Capsaicin is an active ingredient in most hot peppers. It makes your mouth feel like it's burning. You can even feel the burning sensation on your finger if you rub the inside of a hot pepper.

Now, milk has an ingredient called casein. It binds with the capsaicin oil on your tongue or throat and washes it away."

"Well, it would have been nice to know that about an hour ago!" Evan complained.

"Speaking of science projects," Avery chimed in, "I have an idea for one we could do this afternoon."

"What is it?" Roo asked.

"I can't get the words from the clue we found this morning out of my head," Avery said. "Some of the words stuck out to me: silk and sticky."

"Silk, like Mimi's red scarf!" Evan said. "But it's soft and slick. I wouldn't describe silk as sticky."

"Yes, but spider webs are made of spider silk!" Ella chimed in. Her eyes grew wide with understanding. "And spider webs are sticky!"

"Exactly," Avery said. "I think we should engineer a way to study a spider web up close."

"Without studying the spider, right?" Evan asked.

"No spiders allowed," Roo promised. She smiled at Evan as he eyed Fluffy. The tarantula sunbathed in the afternoon light in her glass tank.

"Look at this!" Ella said. She pulled up a search engine on Roo's pink laptop and typed "capturing a spider web."

"I think we have all the supplies for this project around the house," Roo said.

"Let's get to work!" declared Avery.

Roo borrowed hairspray and baby powder from her mom's bathroom. Ella grabbed a black poster board from Professor Clark's office. Avery found a pair of scissors in the kitchen drawer. Evan picked up a magnifying glass off a shelf in the living room.

The kids met on the patio in Roo's backyard, where an aqua umbrella shaded a round table and four metal chairs. A wooden swing set covered with a bright yellow awning sat in the back corner of the yard.

"I saw a big web on the swing set the other morning," Roo said. "It was easy to see because dew stuck to the lines and made them look like strands of tiny pearls."

The kids carried their supplies over to the swing set. "It was right here between the two chains of this swing," Roo said. She pointed to the metal chain holding up one of the bright blue swings.

"It's still there!" Ella cried. "And it looks perfect! No tears!"

"I don't necessarily like spiders," Evan said, "but don't you think this is kind of mean? This web is the spider's home. Where's he going to live if we tear it down for scientific research?"

Roo reached out and gently flicked the silky lines that held the web to the swing chain. It vibrated under her touch.

"The spider must have moved," Roo said with a smile. "When a spider feels vibrations in its web, it rushes toward the movement to ward off predators."

"So this guy moved out?" Evan asked.

"Exactly. Most spiders build new webs every night," Roo answered. "So it doesn't hurt them to take an old web for an experiment."

"As Papa would say, this one's ripe for the pickin'," Ella added in her best Papa impression.

The kids carefully followed the instructions they'd found on the Internet. Avery shook some baby powder into her palm. She gently blew the powder over the web until the lines turned white. Then Roo popped the pink plastic lid off her mom's hairspray and soaked the black poster board until it was sticky with hair product.

"We have to work fast before the hairspray dries," Avery warned.

Roo and Ella carefully **aligned** the black poster so it was centered over the entire spider web. They gently pushed it forward until the web made contact with the sticky hairspray.

"Go, Evan!" Ella yelled. Evan cut the four silk strands that held the web to the swing chains. Roo and Ella pulled back the poster board to see a perfectly shaped spider web!

"It's so beautiful!" Ella said. "It looks like a piece of artwork."

Avery carried the poster board back to the table to let it dry. Roo, Ella, and Evan scooted their chairs together to study the web with the magnifying glass.

"So what do we know about a spider web?" Avery asked.

"It's made of spider silk," Ella said.

"A web is sticky if you walk through it," Evan added.

"It's made of patterned lines in a circle," Roo chimed in.

"Oh, and it's nearly invisible without dew or powder on the web's lines," Ella said.

"Good!" Avery said. "I think I'm beginning to understand 'soft as silk' and 'sticky sweet.' The clue is definitely about a spider web. But the rest of the clue still doesn't make any sense."

"The last clue was about a tarantula, right?" Evan said. Avery nodded. "Then maybe we shouldn't just focus on the web," he added. "Maybe we should look up how spiders use their webs."

Avery raised her eyebrows at her brother's comment. "I think you actually just had a good idea, little bro!"

Ice-cold milk soothes Evan's mouth after eating a hot pepper!

12

SPIDERMAN

"It says here that spiders use their silk for different things like mating, protection, and to catch their dinner," Ella read. She was poring over a spider facts page on the Internet. The kids were back in Roo's bedroom. They huddled on the floor around Avery's iPhone. "Look here! This web was made by an orb-weaver. They build their intricate webs in an hour. The webs have sticky spots to catch insects that accidentally fly through them. The spider then covers the insect in webbing and eats it by sucking out its insides."

"Ewww!" Avery groaned. "Here we go again!"

"That picture looks like the silk is coming out of the spider's bottom!" Evan pointed to the photograph and giggled.

"It actually comes from a gland in its abdomen," Ella continued. "The silk is liquid inside the spider, but turns to a solid as the spider pulls it from its gland. The silk is elastic, but as strong as steel!"

"Everyone knows that," Evan said. "Haven't you ever seen *Spiderman*? He swings off 100-story buildings with that stuff, so it has to be strong!"

"I don't think we can count a movie character who shoots spider silk from his wrists as scientific evidence," Ella said with a sigh.

"Can too!" Evan retorted.

"Stop, you two," Avery said. She stood up suddenly and stared at the clue. "I think I get it. 'Once it's caught, it cannot leave'. The clue must be talking about a spider's prey!"

"Once a bug's caught in the web, it's definitely stuck," Ella said. "I think you're right, Avery!"

"But there's one big problem here," Roo chimed in. "Tarantulas don't build webs to catch prey." She stepped over to Fluffy's glass tank and pointed to the terra cotta pot that served as a burrow. "See how Fluffy put webbing outside her burrow?" she asked.

Avery and Ella examined the thick white covering. Fluffy had woven together multiple layers of thin silk to make a web blanket around the edges of the burrow. She'd fashioned a hole in the center to enter the burrow. Several single strands of silk stretched across the dirt entrance. "Fluffy uses the webbing for protection," Roo explained. "Those strands along the ground vibrate if a predator is near the burrow so Fluffy can hide or attack."

"I may not want to know this, but how do tarantulas find their dinner?" Evan asked.

"The good old-fashioned way," Roo said. "They hunt!"

"So the clue is about spiders, but not necessarily tarantulas," Avery remarked.

"Maybe it doesn't have anything to do with the clue we found at the insect collection," Ella offered.

"But why leave a note in a tarantula trap?" Roo said.

"Trap!" Avery exclaimed. "We found the clue in a tarantula trap that seemed like it was buried for someone to find. It says 'once it's caught, it can't leave.' What does that sound like?"

"Like someone wants to catch a tarantula?" Evan asked.

"Maybe," Avery said. "But it sounds like a threat to me. Like whoever left the clue wants to catch a person!"

"Do you think they want to catch *us*?" Ella asked. She started to wonder if they should be mixed up in this mystery at all. She thought about the man in black peering down the brim of his hat right at her. An eerie feeling made the hair on the back of her neck stand up. *What if the man in black is after us?*

13

ZOO CLUE

Early the next morning, the kids piled into the jeep in front of Roo's house. Ella didn't like being mixed up in a mystery, but she was determined to enjoy her day at the zoo.

"I want to see the giraffes!" Ella exclaimed. "They're my favorite!"

"We've got all morning," Papa said. "Hopefully we can see all the animals!"

Papa parked the jeep and ushered the kids toward the entrance of Tucson's Reid Park Zoo. A white triangular awning shaded the ticket windows from the blazing sun. Swaying palm trees and shrubs lined the outside of the concrete building. Inside the gates, wide pathways wound through various animal exhibits. Each was made to look just like the animal's natural habitat.

Avery grabbed a map from a covered pavilion on the way in. "To our left are the tigers!" she announced. Enormous orange cats with thick black stripes paced around a spacious enclosure filled with grass, dirt, and rock formations. One tiger lounged on the top of a flat boulder. His leg hung off the side and swayed in the breeze. Another rested in the cool green grass and cleaned its ear with a massive paw.

"They act just like giant versions of regular house cats!" Evan said.

"They're actually kind of cute," Avery said.

"Until you see their fangs," Papa joked. "You don't want to cuddle with a tiger!"

The group continued walking along the winding zoo trails. They saw pigs, otters, zebras, lions, and elephants. Avery enjoyed reading the information markers at each enclosure.

"Did you know giraffes only sleep about two hours a day?" Avery asked Ella at the giraffe exhibit. They watched a spotted giraffe crane his neck to the tip top of a tree and use his gray tongue to break off a leafy branch.

"Yep, they only sleep for a short time so they can stay **vigilant** for predators the rest of the day," Ella said. Avery was surprised her little sister knew so much about giraffes.

"I looked them up on the iPad before we got here," Ella confessed. "I told you giraffes are my favorite!"

"I think we've seen just about every animal here," Papa said as they left the giraffe exhibit. "Follow me to the gift shop. I want to get Sadie a souvenir."

"Guys, look!" Ella whispered. Her voice trembled. She pointed toward a green wooden bench in the distance. A man in a dark gray fedora sat on the bench with a newspaper in front of his face.

"See the feather on his hat?" Ella whispered to Avery. "That's got to be him!"

"Hey!" Roo yelled at the man.

"Roo! What are you doing?" Avery cried. The man calmly folded his newspaper and stood up. He stared at Roo with the same look he gave Ella at the insect collection.

Then he slowly walked down a path away from the kids.

"Whewwww!" Roo let out her breath. "I thought if I yelled at him he might leave us alone," she said. "I don't think it worked, though. He really is creepy!"

"We better get back to Papa," Avery said. The kids hurried toward to the gift shop near the zoo exit. Ella was relieved when she saw her grandfather.

"What did you get for Sadie?" she asked. Papa handed her the bag. Ella peered inside and smiled. "It's a pink giraffe! She'll love it!"

"I thought so," Papa said.

Ella reached back inside the bag and pulled out what looked like an extra receipt. She unfolded the piece of paper. Her heart raced. *Was it another clue?* The words were scrawled in the same handwriting as the last clue:

Cite seeing may be cool, but danger waits if you break the rules.

Ella felt sure this clue was a threat, and she knew who wrote it. The man in black was following them and he wasn't trying to hide! *But why would he would want to harm us?*

14

EYES IN THE BACK OF THEIR HEADS

After a quick lunch of fresh fish tacos from a local food truck, Ella was feeling a little better, especially since Papa agreed to take the kids to Henry's Pet Emporium. She was excited to ask to hold a tarantula. Just before the kids arrived at the pet store, Ella slipped Avery the new clue.

"I found this in Papa's bag from the gift shop," she whispered. Avery drew in a sharp breath as she read the menacing words.

"We need to be careful to keep our distance from the man in black," she said. "We can't have another run-in like we had at the zoo. That was too close for comfort."

Ella jumped out of the jeep and followed Papa and Evan into the pet store. Avery lagged behind to show the new clue to Roo.

"You can't confront the man in black again, Roo," Avery warned. "It's too dangerous."

"There's something strange about this clue," Roo said in a distracted voice. "See it? 'Cite' is spelled wrong. It should be S-I-G-H-T."

"I didn't even notice that," Avery said. "I guess our menacing man in black isn't a very good speller."

"No, I don't think that's it," Roo said. "I think it's misspelled intentionally!" She grabbed a pen from her yellow backpack. She rested the paper against her knee and quickly wrote out a word. "C-I-T-E-S—see how it looks capitalized?" Roo said.

"The CITES treaty!" Avery cried. "The spelling *was* intentional!"

"Why would we break the rules of the CITES treaty?" Roo asked. "It doesn't make any sense."

"Are you girls joining us?" Papa asked, leaning his head out of the pet shop's glass door.

Roo stuffed the clue and her pen back in the bag and followed Avery into the pet shop. Inside, the girls noticed an entire wall of glass that looked into a kennel with cats, puppies, rabbits, and small mice tucked into clean, spacious cages. The center of the store was divided into two aisles by a display of animal food, toys, leashes, and collars. Shiny aquariums filled with colorful fish, hermit crabs, and lizards covered the back wall of the store. A couple of aquarium tanks were empty except for brown dirt in the bottom.

"I'm so glad all of you came by!" Henry exclaimed. "I believe I promised you a look at some Arizona critters. Follow me!" He led the kids toward the glass tanks in the back of the shop. A light brown tarantula stood motionless in one of them.

"This is an Arizona blonde tarantula," Henry announced. He pointed to the tank next to it. "And this is—"

"A Mexican red-kneed tarantula!" Ella blurted out.

"Well, you know your spiders!" Henry said.

"I can't really take the credit," Ella said. "Roo taught me just about everything I know."

"Would anyone like to hold one?" Henry asked. "Who's brave enough today?"

"Me!" Ella's hand shot into the air. "I want to hold one!"

"That's my girl!" Papa said, nodding his head in approval.

Evan's eyebrows shot up in surprise. He stepped away from the tarantula tank. Avery bit her lip as Henry reached into the tank and gently grabbed the spider with his bare hand. He directed Ella to hold her hand out flat before he placed it in her palm.

Ella giggled with nerves and excitement. "Ooooh, it feels prickly," she said.

"That's because he's covered in tiny hairs," Henry explained. "Tarantulas also have special bristle hair on their abdomen they can use in defense. When they feel threatened, they lift their back legs and shake hair off their abdomen. Then, they fling the hair at their predator. The tiny bristles, called urticating hairs, stun the enemy."

Ella felt her body tense. "He won't stick me with those hairs, will he?"

"Oh, don't worry," Henry said, noticing Ella's nerves. "He won't do it unless provoked. But even if he did spray you with his urticating hairs, you'd only get a little rash for a couple of hours."

Ella felt her **fortitude** fleeting. "I think I'm done," she said.

Henry carefully lifted the tarantula out of Ella's palm. She noticed something on its head.

"Are all those little black dots its *eyes*?" she asked.

"You got it," Henry replied. "Mexican red-kneed tarantulas have eight eyes on top of their heads."

"And I thought only Mimi had extra eyes in the back of her head," Evan said. "Maybe they're related."

"Evan!" Avery chastised her little brother. Papa let out a booming belly laugh.

"I have a pet Mexican red-kneed tarantula," Roo told Henry proudly.

"That's great!" Henry said. "These little guys make great pets. They're in high demand! I'm actually looking to increase my inventory."

"Roo told us some people capture tarantulas with tarantula traps," Ella said. "Is that how you're getting your new spiders?"

"Oh no, no," Henry replied. He laughed nervously. "I have a special supplier." He changed the subject quickly. "Can I interest you in any pet supplies?"

"I think I'd like to pick up a new stick for Fluffy's pen," Roo said. She picked out a thick, smooth stick that looked like a Y at one end. "She likes to climb sometimes."

Henry led Roo to the checkout counter. "Just be careful not to put this too close to the top of her tank," Henry said. "It could be the perfect escape route!"

While Henry rang up Fluffy's new stick, Avery glanced at a display on the long glass countertop. She noticed a white edge peeking out between two tubs of goldfish food flakes. She carefully scooted the edge out from between the tubs and realized it was a piece of graph paper.

The paper had three columns of handwritten numbers on it. The column headings were *Quantity*, *Price of Spider*, and *Profit*. Avery was just about to offer the piece of paper to Henry when she saw something familiar at the bottom.

Quantity	Price of Spider	Profit
	$250	$12,500

Brachypelma smithi, pronto

"*Brachypelma smithi*, pronto" she whispered softly. "Same as the first clue!"

She slipped the graph paper into her shorts pocket and waved goodbye to Henry as she followed Papa to the jeep.

Did the man in black get to the pet store before we did? Why would he plant a clue in the fish food? Are the numbers some sort of warning, too? Avery's head spun with questions as the evening wind whipped through the jeep's windows and twirled her hair like a tornado.

15

NEST WEB

That night, Roo stayed at the hotel with Avery, Ella, and Evan. While Mimi and Papa stepped out to pick up take-out Chinese food for dinner, the kids spread all the clues on the gold hotel bedspread.

"Spiders, Spanish, threats, and numbers," Avery listed. "These clues don't seem to go together."

"They all have something to do with spiders," Roo offered.

"This page of numbers looks like an inventory list," Avery said. "The total profit is listed as $12,500, but the price of one spider is only $250. That means someone expects to sell 50 spiders. Henry only had one Mexican red-kneed tarantula at his store."

"He did say he was planning to get more," Ella said. "Maybe this is his list."

"But the words at the bottom are just like the first clue," Evan said. "Henry couldn't have left both."

"Yeah, and what about the man in black?" Roo asked. "We know he's the one who left the clue at the zoo. He had to leave these, too."

"It doesn't make any sense." Avery was frustrated **analyzing** the same clues over and over.

"I hope tomorrow is mystery-free," Roo declared. "We get to go to the Arizona-Sonora Desert Museum. Your Papa saved the best stop for last!"

"Museum, snooze-eum," Evan said. "Booooring."

"I think you might actually like this one," Roo said. But Evan was already distracted by the scent of steaming sesame chicken and fried rice that Mimi and Papa carried through the door.

The next morning, Papa and the kids dropped Mimi off at the university to continue her research, and then headed to the museum.

"So much for a relaxing getaway," Papa said. "It's exhausting keeping you kiddos entertained!"

The entrance area of the Arizona-Sonora Desert Museum was housed in a one-story, tan stucco building. Outside the building, wide columns topped with a wooden arbor welcomed guests.

"This place doesn't look very big," Evan said, pleasantly surprised. He was excited to dodge a boring day looking at artifacts in a museum.

"That's because most of the museum is outside!" Roo said. "There are 21 acres of walking paths here."

Papa let out an exhausted sigh, but put on a brave smile. "I may have to sit this one out," he remarked.

"Don't worry, Papa," Avery said. "I see some very comfy seating over there." She pointed toward two wooden benches just inside the museum.

"That's where you'll find me," Papa said. "Roo, you're in charge since you know your way around." He made a beeline for the benches, but not before he told the kids to be careful and to text him to check in.

"This place has hundreds of different types of native animals and over a thousand varieties of desert plants," Roo explained as she led the kids down one of the museum trails.

"I thought nothing could grow in the desert," Evan said. "Isn't it just hills of sand as far as the eye can see?"

"Oh, no," Roo replied. "The Sonoran Desert actually has vibrant plant life. The museum shows how plants and animals have **codependent** relationships in the desert. It really is like no place else in the world!"

"I want to check out the hummingbird aviary," Avery said. She pointed toward a small building with no roof and mesh caging spread over the top. Avery spied hummingbirds furiously flapping their tiny wings inside.

"They beat their wings so fast, you can't even see them!" Avery exclaimed. Ella pulled up a fact sheet about hummingbirds on the iPhone.

"So that's where the name hummingbird comes from," Ella said. "Their wings make a humming sound when they fly."

"They kind of look like glorified bumble bees to me!" Evan observed.

"Actually, they are the tiniest birds in the world!" Roo read from a sign outside the building.

"Hey, I've got a fascinating fact for you guys!" Ella said. "Why do hummingbirds like spiders?"

"Because their brains are too tiny to know any better?" Evan offered.

"It's because hummingbirds use spider webs!" Ella said. "Look!" The kids crowded around an informational plaque on the outside wall of the aviary.

"When they first opened the aviary, there were no spiders around," Ella read. "The hummingbirds' nests kept falling apart. The museum workers couldn't figure out what was wrong until they realized that hummingbirds use spider webs to hold their nests together!

"The workers gathered up spider webs from around the museum," she continued, "and placed them in the aviary. The hummingbirds used the webbing to strengthen their nests and the problem was solved!"

"Hey! Guys! What's th-th-th-that?" Avery stuttered.

Ella and Roo turned to see Avery frozen in place. Ella knew something was seriously wrong. She looked in the direction of Avery's stare, expecting to see the man in black. Then, she saw it. A massive, menacing brown cloud stretched from the ground to the sky as wide as her eyes could see. It was rolling like a tsunami wave, right toward them!

16

DUST RUSH

"It's a haboob!" Roo yelled.

"A WHAT?" Evan asked. His eyes were glued to the hummingbirds.

"Haboob! It's a REALLY big dust storm!" Roo yelled. "We have to take cover. Fast!"

Evan whirled around to see the ominous cloud building in the distance.

"AHHHH!" Evan screamed. He grabbed Avery's arm, digging his nails into her skin.

The cloud boiled toward the museum like a whirling brown wall. It looked as if would swallow them alive! The kids raced to the museum building where Papa was snoozing on the bench. They flung open the glass doors and hustled inside.

"Papa! Papa!" the kids yelled.

Papa pushed his cowboy hat back on his head. "Done already?" he asked.

"Papa, we have to take cover, it's coming for us," Evan cried between heaving breaths. "It looks really bad. I don't know if we're going to make it!" Evan grabbed Papa's arm and yanked him up from the bench in a frenzy.

"Calm down, Evan," Roo said. "We *have* taken cover. We're perfectly safe inside the building."

"That giant cloud wall looks like it will knock this building down without a second thought," Avery said. She didn't blame her brother for being scared.

"It looks bad, but it's just dust and sand," Roo explained. "Haboobs happen from time to time around here."

"How does that thing get started?" Ella asked. She peeked out the glass doors with confidence now that she knew they were all safe.

"It starts when heavy winds from a severe thunderstorm blow up dust from the desert floor," Roo explained. "The dust mixes with the wind and forms a dust wall thousands of feet high. It's kind of like a snowball that keeps getting bigger as it rolls down a mountain. The haboob gathers more and more dust and becomes stronger and bigger as it travels."

"What happens to the people who are caught outside or driving on the road?" Avery asked. She was still alarmed by the impending cloud rolling in like smoke from a huge fire.

"Most people around here know to take shelter," Roo said. "Cars pull over to the side of the road and wait for it to pass. It just leaves a layer of sand on everything."

"The JEEP!" Papa boomed. "Oh no! The windows are open!" Papa looked out the window at the front parking lot just in time to see the giant sand cloud envelop his rental car. And before they knew it, the whole building was engulfed in a haze of sand and wind. The dust was so thick Avery couldn't see the stucco columns right outside the glass doors.

The kids tried to distract themselves by watching time-lapse videos of haboobs on Avery's iPhone. Video after video showed giant sandstorms appearing to swallow entire cities as they rumbled across the landscape.

Soon, bits of blue sky peeked through the dreary clouds. A layer of dust and sand smothered the sidewalk and museum signs. A coating almost an inch thick covered the jeep's seats and floorboards.

"I think we're going to have to cut this visit short, unfortunately," Papa said. "We've got to get the jeep cleaned up before we pick up Mimi. We all have a long day tomorrow at the Insect Festival!"

Papa and the kids brushed the sand off their seats and headed toward the closest carwash. "I think I'm going to have sand in my pants for a year after this," Evan said. He shifted uncomfortably in his seat. Roo, Ella, and Avery giggled.

I'm thankful we're safe after all we've been through, Avery thought. *Who knows what tomorrow will bring?!*

17

ARACHNOPHOBIA

The next morning, the whole crew loaded up in the freshly cleaned jeep and headed for the Forbes Building.

"I've learned such amazing things about Arizona insects this week!" Mimi told the kids from the front seat. "Did you kids know that a female tarantula can lay hundreds of eggs at one time?" Mimi turned and winked at Evan. "I thought you might like that creepy crawly fact."

"Mimi, I know more than I *ever* wanted to know about tarantulas!" Evan declared. "In fact, I don't think I need to know one more thing about those beastly things." He shook his head slowly in exasperation.

"It's OK, Evan," Mimi said. "I understand!"

"I think tarantulas are cool, Mimi," Ella piped up.

"Our brave little Ella held a real live tarantula the other day at the pet store," Papa said proudly.

"Really?" Mimi said. "I wish I'd seen that! I've missed quite a lot being away from you all. I'm glad you'll be at the university with me today."

"You are going to *love* the Insect Festival," Roo said. "I go there every year!

This year we're going to help Professor Clark with the arachnid table," Mimi told the kids.

Evan grimaced. "I just can't get away from those things," he grumbled.

When they arrived at the Forbes Building, faculty members and entomology students bustled about setting up festival displays and booths.

"Go ahead and look around before everyone gets here," Professor Clark suggested. A myriad of fascinating insect displays packed the room from corner to corner. The kids' eyes darted from gorgeous butterflies and big black beetles to plump caterpillars and skinny brown stick insects.

Avery wandered to a table with a box of caterpillars as blue as the Arizona desert sky.

"Want to hold one?" a friendly student asked.

Avery hesitated. "Caterpillars don't have fangs, do they?" she asked.

"Nope!" he replied.

"OK, then, I will," Avery said. The caterpillar was about as thick and long as her pointer finger. It inched its way across her palm, slowly scrunching the middle of its body, then stretching it out again. It felt smooth and soft against her hand.

Evan eyed a row of computers on a table across the room with bright red, round glasses lying beside them. He decided a computer was the safest place to visit at an insect festival—no slime, stingers, or fangs! A student showed Evan how to use the glasses to view the world like a bug would as it crawled along the ground.

Ella headed for a display with a wide, shallow box filled with bright green

Astroturf. Little lines were spaced along the green surface like white lines on a football field. An entomology professor picked up two large beetles and set them down on one side of the "field."

"Cheer them on!" she told Ella.

Ella walked to the opposite side of the box and giggled as the beetles slowly crept toward her.

"Come on," Ella urged. "You can do it!" A black beetle with red wings moved ahead of a fat brown one with two long horns on his head.

"I think Red Wings is gonna win!" Ella said. As Ella's choice scurried across the last white line, the professor grabbed it and lifted it high in the air.

"Skeetle the Beetle is our first Beetle Bowl champion of the day!" she announced to the room. Onlookers standing near Ella cheered and applauded.

At the arachnid table, Roo peered through the lenses of a big black **microscope**. She stared through two cylinders, like a pair of binoculars. A dozen tiny tarantula eggs lay on a glass plate below the microscope lenses.

The tiny balls looked like opaque yellow beads. Roo used the microscope to magnify the eggs so she could see every detail. She secretly hoped she might see a baby tarantula hatch!

The rest of the arachnid table included a display of big and small spiders, a section where kids could make their own spiders out of play dough and pipe cleaners, and a clear tank at the end of the table with a live tarantula lurking inside.

The doors to the insect festival opened at 11:00 a.m. sharp. Chattering adults and children poured in, scattering to the different tables like ants at a picnic. People took turns touching beetles, examining brightly colored butterflies, and studying insects through the microscopes placed around the room.

At the arachnid table, Evan helped kids form the two sections of a spider out of green modeling clay. Then, he offered his "students" bright red pipe cleaners to use for spider legs. Avery and Roo helped guests with the microscopes and answered questions about the spider displays.

Ella stayed busy at the live tarantula tank. Professor Clark placed the spider in the hands of parents and kids while Ella urged them not to be afraid. She even held the tarantula to demonstrate that there was nothing to worry about.

After a couple of hours, Avery took a break. She rode the elevator to the ground floor and headed for the water fountains next to a glass door at the rear of the building. As she pulled her blond hair back to take a sip, she noticed a large cardboard box outside the door.

Avery opened the door and squatted down beside the box. The address line was made out to the University of Arizona Entomology Department. Avery had a feeling Professor Clark would be expecting the package. She decided to carry it back upstairs to save him the trip.

Roo met Avery in the hallway outside the bustling insect festival.

"Is that a package for my dad?" she asked.

"I don't know, I found it outside the door at the back of the building." Avery hoisted the box into Roo's arms.

"This has to be it!" Roo said. "Dad is expecting a new insect display for his office. He's adding a tarantula. Let's open it for him as a surprise!"

Avery grabbed Ella and Evan from the arachnid table and promised Mimi they'd be right back to help.

"Roo's dad got a new insect display today," Avery explained to her brother and sister. "We want to surprise him by setting it up in his office while he's distracted."

The kids gathered around the big box on top of Professor Clark's cluttered desk. Roo carefully cut open the packing tape.

"I can't wait to see this tarantula!" she exclaimed. She pulled the flaps of the box back to find not one tarantula, but dozens of baby tarantulas—very much alive and crawling all over the white packing peanuts inside the box!

A tarantula fits nicely in a person's hand!

18

TARANTULA SNATCHA'

"AAHHHH!" Avery screamed. Evan and Roo jumped back in shock. Ella stood frozen in fear as hundreds of hairy legs crept along the sides of the box. Evan shut the top of the box, and smothered it with tape.

"I...am...not...touching...a...tarantula... today!" Evan cried. BOOM! BOOM! He urgently stacked heavy science books on top of the box.

"Evan," Ella yelled. "EVAN!" Evan stopped and looked at his sister. "You can stop now! I don't think the spiders are getting out!" she observed. Evan suddenly realized he was standing on top of Professor Clark's desk. The box of creepy crawly spiders had at least ten textbooks piled on top of it.

"This doesn't make sense," Roo said. "I know my dad didn't order these!"

Ella ripped a packing slip out of a plastic pouch on the side of the box. "Quantity: L Tarantulas," she read.

"Maybe it stands for Live Tarantulas," Roo suggested.

"But it says 'quantity'," Ella said. "It should say how many, right?"

"Maybe it's a Roman numeral," Avery said. Suddenly, the clues started to fall into place. "The Roman numeral L stands for 50!"

"Just like the inventory list?" Evan asked.

"Exactly," Avery declared. "And the spiders in that box were Mexican red-kneed tarantulas. I saw the red on their legs. I have to get back downstairs!" She raced toward the elevator with the other kids close behind.

When Avery reached the back door where she had found the package, she noticed a man in a white polo shirt and dark pants walking down the sidewalk, away from the door. She opened the door on a whim and shouted.

"Hey, you!" The man turned around. She expected to see the man in black, but she saw another familiar face instead.

"Mr. Henry?" Avery said, startled. "What are you doing here?"

"Oh, uh, I just got lost again," Henry replied. He looked around nervously. Instead of his usual friendly smile, a scowl spread across his face. "Umm, you didn't see a package here, did you?"

Avery knew then it was Henry all along.

"The box of spiders was supposed to be for you!" Avery said. It was hard to believe the friendly pet store owner was the culprit. Henry whirled and started running toward the side of the building.

"He's getting away!" Roo yelled. The four kids dashed after Henry.

"We'll never catch him if he gets to his car!" Avery said.

19

SUSPECTS, SMUGGLERS, AND SPIDERS...OH MY!

The kids rounded the corner only to see Henry thrashing his arms and legs like a jumbo-sized tarantula. He was pinned to the ground by a tall man wearing a dark gray fedora!

"The man in black!" Ella screamed. She watched as he snapped handcuffs around Henry's wrists and yanked him off the ground.

"I know you've been following us," Ella said. She felt brave. She wasn't going to let Henry or the man in black get away. "You can't mess with us anymore! I'm calling the police!" Ella pulled out her cell phone and started to dial 9-1-1.

"There's no need to do that," the man in black said. "You just helped save the Mexican red-kneed tarantula from further danger. I'm on your side."

Ella pulled the phone away from her ear and hit the red "End Call" button. "But you threatened to hurt us!" she said.

"I never wanted to hurt you," the man in black said. "I'm Agent Sawyer from the U.S. Fish and Wildlife Service. My job is to find people breaking the CITES treaty by illegally importing endangered and fragile species. We had a tip that someone was importing Mexican red-kneed tarantulas to the university."

"You planted the tarantula trap at the horse stable!" Avery shouted.

"You're right," Agent Sawyer admitted. "And the note at the zoo. I thought Roo's father might be involved in the illegal trade so I was watching him closely. When his daughter had three friends come in from out of town, I thought you might be here to buy a tarantula as a pet illegally. I wanted to warn you so you didn't break the law!"

"You thought *I* wanted to buy a tarantula?" Evan said.

"I had to be sure," Agent Sawyer said. "I didn't just follow you to make sure you weren't involved. I also wanted to protect you. Once I figured out Henry McGee was the real suspect, I wanted make sure you kids were safe from him."

"How did you find out it was Henry?" Ella asked. "He seemed so nice!" Henry was trying to wiggle his arms out of the handcuffs with no success.

"I was following a lead the day you saw me in the U of A insect collection," Agent Sawyer said. "Someone tipped me off that Henry had been studying the tarantula display and looked suspicious. I started following you kids and him. I realized Henry wanted to import the tarantulas illegally so he could make a lot of money by selling them. It wasn't long before I had enough proof to take him down."

"I found this at the insect collection," Avery said. She pulled the first clue from her pocket. Henry huffed in frustration at the evidence.

"That's Henry's handwriting, all right," Agent Sawyer said. "It looks like he was trying to find the right Spanish words to communicate with the smugglers down in Mexico."

"He must have written the scientific name for Mexican red-kneed tarantulas to make sure he got the right kind of spider in his shipment," Evan said.

"So that's what we found in the pet shop!" Ella remembered the graph paper with the columns of numbers. "It *was* Henry's inventory list."

"And I was going to make a fortune off those spiders, too! I should never have stopped to ask you kids for directions!" Henry growled.

"Why did you have delivered the tarantulas here?" Roo asked Henry.

"The day I saw you kids, I was looking for a safe place for my shipment of tarantulas to be delivered," Henry replied. "Once I talked to you, I knew your dad was the perfect cover up." He snarled through his teeth when he spoke. "I couldn't send the shipment to my pet store without getting caught. I figured people would think it was for the university's scientific research if I had it shipped here. No one would know they were for me. It was a perfect plan until you kids messed up everything!"

"What's going on out here?" Mimi and Papa ran around the corner. Mimi gathered the kids into her arms. "Are you all OK?"

"Everything's fine here, ma'am," Agent Sawyer said. "These kids saved the day!"

Agent Sawyer called the police to come get Henry for further questioning. He glared at the kids as two muscular officers stuffed him into the police car.

"We'll make sure he comes to justice," Agent Sawyer assured them. He explained the situation to Mimi, Papa, and Professor Clark.

Professor Clark retrieved the box of baby tarantulas and gave them to Agent Sawyer. "These little guys will be released back into their native habitat in Mexico," he explained. "They will get to live long lives because of your bravery."

"Will they be safe from smugglers once you release them?" Ella said.

"We'll do our best to keep anyone from stealing them from their natural habitat,"

Agent Sawyer assured her. "And thanks for that quick thinking on your part, Evan," he added. "You sealed up that box and kept those little guys from escaping!"

"Just what we need in this world—more tarantulas!" Evan rolled his eyes, but deep down, he felt happy to help save the amazing arachnids.

The next day, safely tucked into her seat on the *Mystery Girl*, Avery peeked at her brother and sister sleeping peacefully on their way home. She was relieved that the baby tarantulas had been saved. She would miss Roo, and had promised to write her as often as she could.

But as they flew high over Tucson, with a vibrant purple, orange, and gold sunset behind them, Avery knew she wouldn't miss tarantulas—not even a little!

The End

DO YOU LIKE MYSTERIES?

You have the chance to solve them!
You can solve little mysteries,
like figuring out
how to do your homework and
why your dog always hides your shoes.

You can solve big mysteries, like how to
program a fun computer game,
protect an endangered animal,
find a new energy source,
INVENT A NEW WAY TO DO SOMETHING, explore
outer space, and more!

You may be surprised to find
that *science*, **technology**,
engineering, math, and even
HISTORY, literature, and
ART can help you solve all kinds of
"mysteries" you encounter.

So feed your curiosity, learn all you can, apply
your creativity, and **be a mystery-solver too!**

– Carole Marsh

**More about the Science, Technology,
Engineering, & Math in this book**

DIAGRAM OF MEXICAN RED-KNEED TARANTULA

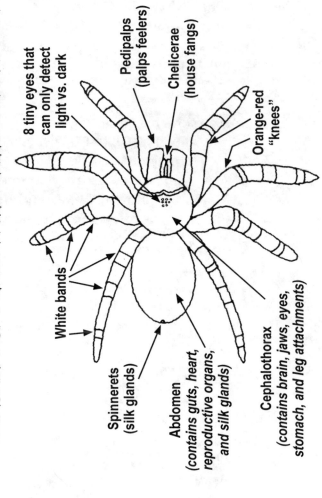

8 tiny eyes that can only detect light vs. dark

Pedipalps (palps feelers)

Chelicerae (house fangs)

Orange-red "knees"

White bands

Spinnerets (silk glands)

Abdomen (contains guts, heart, reproductive organs, and silk glands)

Cephalothorax (contains brain, jaws, eyes, stomach, and leg attachments)

TARANTULA FACTS

1. Tarantulas shed their skin every couple of years through a process called molting. When they molt, they can replace internal organs, stomach lining, and even regrow legs that have been injured or cut off!

2. A tarantula can live off one large meal for up to a month!

3. Female tarantulas sometimes kill and eat male tarantulas after they mate.

4. Female tarantulas can live thirty years or longer in the wild, while male tarantulas only live about seven years on average.

5. The Goliath Bird-Eating Spider is a tarantula with a leg span of almost twelve inches—that's the size of a dinner plate! It lives in South America and can catch and eat birds!

6. Tarantulas have a delicate exoskeleton that can break easily from a fall. Responsible pet owners must be very careful not to drop tarantulas.

7. People in Cambodia, a country in southeast Asia, eat tarantulas fried in butter as a snack!

8. Arachnophobia is a fear of spiders. It is one of the most common phobias.

9. Scientists have identified more than 800 species of tarantulas!

10. Although tarantulas have eight eyes, they have very poor eyesight!

DIFFERENCES BETWEEN INSECTS AND ARACHNIDS

- An insect's body has three segments; an arachnid's body only has two segments.
- Insects have six legs; arachnids have eight legs.
- Insects have compound eyes made up of many repeating units; arachnids have simple eyes.
- Insects have antennae; arachnids do not.
- Many insects have wings; arachnids do not have wings.
- Insects have mandibles (jaws); arachnids have chelicerae (fang-like appendages).
- Insects undergo some form of metamorphosis; arachnids do not.

ETYMOLOGY

The term *arachnid* comes from an ancient Greek legend. In the legend, a woman named Arachne boasted that her weaving was better than anyone else's, including the Greek goddess Athena. This angered Athena, so she turned Arachne into a spider that could only weave webs for itself.

CONVERT CENTIMETERS TO INCHES

To convert centimeters to inches:	To convert inches to centimeters:
multiply number of centimeters by 0.3937007	multiply number of inches by 2.54

~~~~~~~~~~~~~~~~~~~~

HOW TO MAKE A PITFALL TARANTULA TRAP

A pitfall trap is an easy way to capture a tarantula. If you have seen a tarantula in a particular area, set up your trap there. Since tarantulas are nocturnal and roam around at night, create your trap before nightfall.

You'll need just a few things: a garden trowel, empty soup can, leaves, and twigs.

1. Use the garden trowel to dig a hole just the right size for a soup can.

2. Place the soup can into the hole. Make sure that the top of the can is level with the surface of the ground. You don't want any ridges sticking up that could be detected by the spider.

3. Spread a thin layer of leaves, twigs, and other natural items to cover the opening of the can.

4. If you find a tarantula in your trap (or any other critter!), ask an adult for help getting it out!

SLOW GROWER

Saguaro cacti take a very long time to grow. The size of the plant is the main indicator of its age. Saguaro cacti can live a very long time, too—about 150 to 200 years!

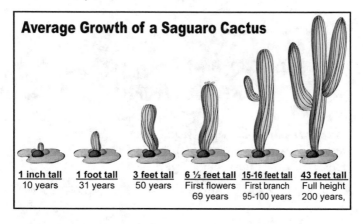

Average Growth of a Saguaro Cactus

1 inch tall	1 foot tall	3 feet tall	6 ½ feet tall	15-16 feet tall	43 feet tall
10 years	31 years	50 years	First flowers 69 years	First branch 95-100 years	Full height 200 years,

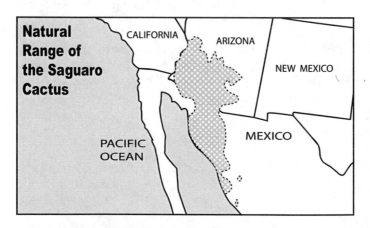

Natural Range of the Saguaro Cactus

CALIFORNIA

ARIZONA

NEW MEXICO

PACIFIC OCEAN

MEXICO

AMAZING SPIDER SILK

Spider webs are made from silk produced by special glands in the spider's abdomen. The silk is actually a protein with amazing strength and elasticity.

Spider silk is incredibly durable. In fact, webs made by *Nephila* orb weaver spiders are so strong that native people in Papua New Guinea use them as handheld fishing nets! Spider silk is considered to be the strongest natural fabric known to man. Ounce for ounce, spider silk is five times stronger than steel!

For many years, scientists and researchers have been working on making a synthetic spider silk in laboratories. They believe it could have an unlimited number of incredible uses, from bulletproof vests to medical products like artificial ligaments and the thread used for stitches!

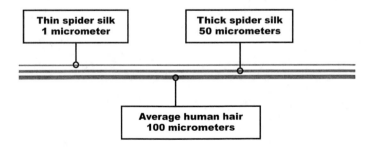

Thin spider silk
1 micrometer

Thick spider silk
50 micrometers

Average human hair
100 micrometers

GLOSSARY

aligned – placed or arranged in a straight line

SAY analyzing – examining something to find out what it is or what makes it work

barricade – a barrier made for protection against attack, or to block the way

SAY bilingual – describes a person who can speak two languages fluently

carcass – the body of a dead animal, or the inner structure of something

cephalothorax – the anterior section of arachnids and many crustaceans, consisting of the fused head and thorax

codependent – depending on others to survive (such as plants or animals in an ecosystem)

cylindrical – having the shape of a cylinder, which is a solid geometric figure with long, straight sides and circular ends of equal size

SAY dismount – to get off a horse, bicycle, or other thing that one is riding

SAY docile – easily taught, led, or controlled

ecosystem – the whole group of living and nonliving things that make up an environment and affect each other

SAY entomology – the branch of science that deals with the study of insects

fedora – a low, soft felt hat with a curled brim and the crown creased lengthwise

SAT fortitude – mental strength and courage that allows someone to face danger, pain, etc.

import – to bring a product into a country to be sold

SAT intricate – having many closely combined parts or elements

SAT menacing – showing intention to commit harm; threatening

metric system – a decimal system of units based on the meter as a unit length and the kilogram as a unit mass

microscope – an optical instrument used for viewing very small objects, such as plant or animal cells, typically magnified several hundred times

overpopulates – fills an area with an excess number of something (usually people) that strains available resources

SAT protruding – sticking out; projecting

provoked – caused a reaction or emotion in someone or something, typically a strong or unwelcome one

scientific name – the recognized Latin name given to an organism, consisting of genus and species

trough – a long, narrow open container for animals to eat or drink out of

SAT vigilant – keeping careful watch for dangers or difficulties

winced – drew back or tensed the body as from pain or from a blow

Enjoy this exciting excerpt from:

THE MYSTERY AT

DOLPHIN COVE

1

DOLPHIN TRAIN

Avery shoved her long blond hair behind her ears and arched her head back. She closed her eyes lazily, and let the sun shine on her face.

"Now, this is what I call a great first week of summer vacation," she said with a yawn.

"It sure is," agreed her younger sister Ella, gazing across the wide May River gently rolling past them.

Dressed in blue denim shorts and t-shirts, the girls perched on the end of a boat dock, its planks gray and worn from years of scorching sunshine and pounding storms. Their bare feet dangled over the edge. The rippling waves of a rising tide tickled their toes.

White sandbars glistened in the hot sun. Islands of tall, chartreuse **marsh** grass dotted the water. Palmetto trees swayed in the warm breeze.

"Look!" said Ella, pointing. Avery opened one eye to see an osprey swoop down to pluck a fish from the rippling water before soaring back up into the cloudless blue sky.

"I'm so glad Mimi and Papa moved here," said Avery, as her open eyelid fluttered shut.

The tall bluffs of Palmetto Bluff, South Carolina, rose up behind them. The girls, along with their mother, father, younger brother Evan, and baby Sadie, were visiting

Mimi and Papa, their grandparents. Their cousin Christina had driven from Savannah to spend a few days with the family, too. Christina attended the Savannah School of Art and Design, known as SCAD.

The kids always had fun with Mimi and Papa! Mimi wrote children's mysteries. She and Papa traveled the world as she researched facts for her books. Avery, Ella, and Evan often got to tag along with their grandparents to **intriguing** new places!

Mimi said their new home in Palmetto Bluff was giving her **inspiration** for lots of new mysteries. And right now, dressed in a scarlet swimsuit and big floppy hat, Mimi sat in the bow of Papa's boat, the *Mimi*, tapping away on her laptop.

Suddenly, Evan, who was perched nearby on the dock, yanked his fishing line from the water.

"ARRRGGGGHH!" he screamed, "something keeps stealing my bait!"

Startled, Avery jumped. "Evan!" she yelled, her eyes flying open. "You scared me to death!"

Just then, a huge gray blur of fish and fin flashed in the water beneath Ella's toes.

"Yikes!" screamed Ella, scrambling to her feet. "It's a shark!" Stumbling and losing her balance, she tumbled into the murky river water.

"That's a dolphin!" yelled Avery, catching a glimpse of the intruder. She ignored her sister splashing in the water. "Look at it go!"

Christina threw down her book and sprang from her seat on the dock. Grabbing her binoculars, she peered at the dolphin quickly gliding away. "Cool! It IS a dolphin!" She extended her hand to help a spewing and sputtering Ella climb up the dock ladder. Soppy wet strands of long blond hair clung to Ella's face. Blades of marsh grass stuck like leeches to her pink t-shirt.

"What's the **commotion**?" hollered Papa, scrambling from the cabin of the *Mimi*. "Is everyone OK?"

"You missed it, Papa," said Evan, his sky-blue eyes twinkling with excitement. "We saw a dolphin, and Ella thought she was shark bait!"

"Ella just swam with a dolphin, so to speak!" Christina added. She pulled a green-and-white striped towel from her beach bag and tossed it to her little cousin.

"Look!" shouted Ella. She pointed across the river. "What's that?"

In the distance, a graceful dolphin leaped out of the water and dove back in just as another popped up.

"There's a sister dolphin," Christina said, "or maybe a mama!"

"I think there are four!" shouted Ella, as the dolphins swam steadily in a straight line down the river.

"It's like a dolphin train!" Avery exclaimed.

"Papa, what's that creepy old boat following them?" asked Ella.

"It looks like an old fishing boat or kind of like a shrimp boat, but different," said Papa. He pushed his black cowboy hat back off his forehead and squinted at the boat in the distance. "See? It has booms out to the side with nets hanging on them."

"It looks like a ghost boat, Captain!" said Evan, saluting his grandpa.

"It looks to me like it's going to run right over those dolphins!" said Avery worriedly.

"I would love to see a dolphin close up," Ella added, her eyes still glued to the animals as they disappeared from view.

"You just did, Ella!" yelled Evan, giggling as he hurled his fishing line back into the water.

"Yes, but I thought it was a shark!" replied Ella. "I was scared. I didn't enjoy it. There's a difference!"

"Do you want to see one of my favorite things?" Christina asked the girls. She held out a delicate, silver chain from around her neck. "This is my dolphin necklace. I wear it all the time."

"Oooooh! It's beautiful!" Ella said.

The silver dolphin, decorated with blue gemstones and a darker blue eye, sparkled in the sun.

"A lot of **symbolism** surrounds dolphins," said Christina.

"What do you mean?" asked Ella.

"Dolphins represent playfulness, gentleness, happiness, and balance," replied Christina. "Lots of people believe dolphins work together to bring harmony and peace to the ocean.

"In ancient Greece," she continued, "the dolphin represented Apollo, the sun god, Artemis, the moon goddess, and Aphrodite, the goddess of love. Greek legend says that dolphins were responsible for carrying souls of the dead to the Islands of the Blessed."

Evan's head snapped around. "That's spooky!" he said.

"I think it's beautiful!" Christina disagreed.

"We need to learn more about dolphins," said Ella.

"Let's make this 'The Summer of the Dolphin,'" Avery added.

"I'm in!" said Evan.

Suddenly, something tugged hard on Evan's fishing line. "WHOA!" he yelled.

SPLASH! Evan tumbled into the waist-high river water. Christina ran to him as he waved his scrawny arms and shook water from his stick-straight blond hair. "OK, I'll pull you up, too," she grumbled and tugged her cousin back onto the dock.

"Fish and bait are now in Davy Jones' Locker!" said Papa with a laugh.

"You're IN, all right!" shouted Ella. Everyone laughed as Ella grabbed her iPod from her backpack and took a selfie of the soaked, smiling duo—she and her brother.

Avery scanned the river. She could no longer see the dolphins, but could still make out the boat following them. She frowned, deep in thought.

Mimi, who hadn't said a word during all the **hoopla**, observed Avery's concerned face and typed: *A ghost ship appeared on the horizon... and the summer would never be the same....*

2

A PIG IN A GHOST BOAT

The kids were lined up, like birds on a telephone wire, on the thick rope hammock that hung between two **gnarled** live oak trees. They **devoured** the turkey and cheese sandwiches that Mimi made for lunch.

Evan licked his fingers. "Mimi makes a gooood sandwich," he said. "But I could've used a little more mayo on mine!" He licked creamy mayonnaise from his fingers and wiped them on his red plaid swim trunks.

"You do like a little turkey and cheese with your mayo, don't you?" said Ella.

Christina munched on a chunky chocolate chip cookie as she read her book. She was happy to spend a few days with her cousins at Mimi and Papa's house before going back to SCAD for summer classes. She loved the **Lowcountry** landscape and the peacefulness of the coast.

"Check out this illustration of things that grow under a pier," said Christina. She held up her book, *Tideland Treasures*. "Here are acorn barnacles, mussels, a starfish, an **anemone**, a finger sponge, a blue crab, and sea pork!"

"Sea pork," chortled Evan. He dashed over to the dock, waded into the marsh muck, and peered beneath the dock. "I don't see any pigs under here!"

The girls giggled. Evan scampered back to the hammock. He beamed. He loved to make the girls laugh. He didn't even have to work that hard to do it!

"I've been thinking," Evan said as he climbed back into the hammock. "Are you sure that wasn't a purpose that almost ate Ella? We drew pictures of purposes in school last year."

"Do you mean a *porpoise*?" asked Christina, grabbing onto the swaying hammock.

"Ba-Bam!" shouted Evan, swinging the hammock harder. "That's what I mean!"

"I know there are lots of dolphins in this river," said Christina, "and all along the Atlantic Coast. But I don't really know how to explain the difference between a dolphin and a porpoise."

"Search it up, Avery!" Evan ordered in his best professor voice.

Avery reached into her green paisley backpack and pulled out her iPhone. "What's the difference between a dolphin and a porpoise?" she asked the phone's personal assistant program. Immediately, a browser page popped up.

"Dolphins and porpoises are marine mammals and closely related to whales," Avery read aloud. "Both are extremely intelligent. Dolphins are generally longer and leaner than porpoises. Dolphins have a curved dorsal fin. Porpoises have a triangular fin, somewhat like a shark's fin. Dolphins have bigger mouths and longer snouts than porpoises. Dolphins are very social and less fearful of humans. Porpoises are shy."

"So dolphins probably like a good party, and porpoises would rather stay home and watch TV," Evan said.

Ella giggled. "Let's go to the sandbar!" she said. "Maybe we'll see some more dolphins!"

"And maybe we'll see the *ghost boat*," Evan said, trying to sound spooky.

The kids sprang out of the hammock. It was still swinging madly when they grabbed their paddle boards and stepped into the river.

"Hey, Papa!" Christina yelled. "We're going to the sandbar. Ella wants to look for more dolphins!"

The kids paddled away from the dock. Papa waved from the *Mimi*. They heard his deep voice singing, "Shrimp boats is a-comin'...their sails are in sight, shrimp boats is a-comin...there's dancin' tonight..."

Avery stood on her orange board and paddled slowly. *"Shrimp boats is a-comin',"* she sang in her head. *"Ghost boats is a-comin'..." That's creepy,* she thought. Then she thought about the dolphins gliding down the river in front of the old boat. *Maybe we will see the dolphins again! After all, THIS is "The Summer of the Dolphin"!*

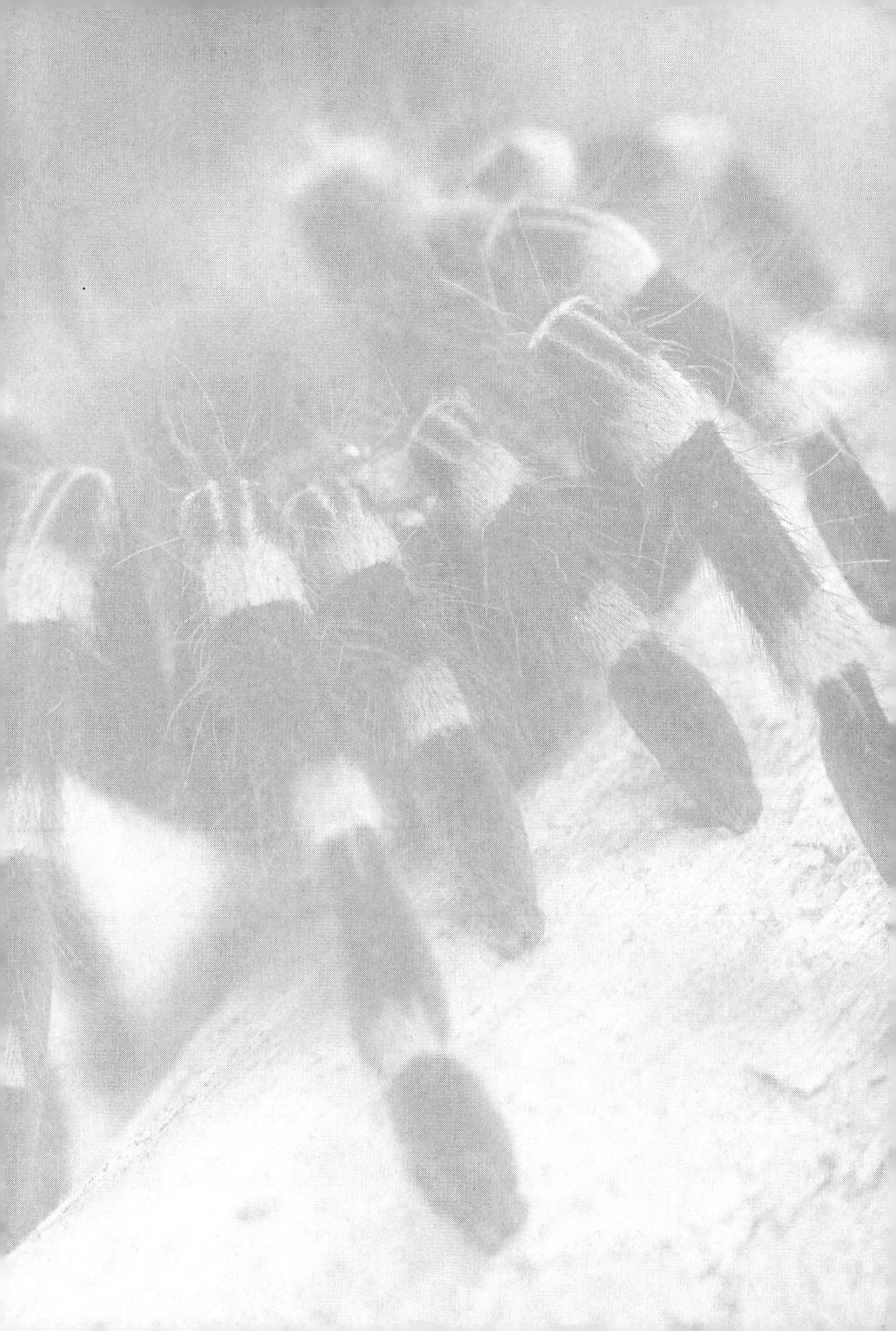